D1111099

LOOSE ENDS

LOOSE ENDS

Murder in the New Jersey Suburbs

A NOVEL BY

DAVID B. WATTS

LICENSED PRIVATE INVESTIGATOR

REALLY!

MILL CITY PRESS

Mill City Press, Inc.
2301 Lucien Way #415
Maitland, FL 32751
407.339.4217
www.millcitypress.net

© 2017 by David B. Watts

All rights reserved. No part of this publication may be reproduced, stored in a retrieval system, or transmitted, in any form or by any means, electronic, mechanical, photocopying, recording, or otherwise, without the prior written permission of the author.

Printed in the United States of America

ISBN: 9781545613528

The New Jersey municipalities and counties mentioned in this book are all real, as are some of the various restaurants and other businesses within those locations. The author's purpose is to inject a sense of realism in terms of setting... nothing further is intended, nor implied.

Robert Higgins is a real-life New Jersey private detective. He and his wife, Brenda, graciously allowed—no— encouraged the author to include them in this novel. Bob Higgins and the author have collaborated for more than twenty-five years on many real-life investigation cases. We're still at it.

The book's protagonist, Claude Frederick "Mack" Mackey, was a real-life person until his untimely passing in 1972. He was not a private detective. He was a quiet, hard-working, loving man who became stepfather to my wife, Linda, until pancreatic cancer took him away. All these years he has been missed dearly, so the author is honoring his memory by using his name as one of the lead characters. Anyone who knew Mack would approve. So would he.

In all other facets, however, this book is a work of fiction. Names, characters, incidents and places are creations of the author's imagination and any resemblance to actual persons, living or dead, or to actual events is unintentional and coincidental.

CHAPTER
One

In action, be primitive; in foresight, a strategist.

René Char – Poet and member of French Resistance

Monday, 4:25 p.m. — New Providence, New Jersey

*A*s always—taking security precautions—he stashed his van in the lot of the adjoining office building and walked the short distance to the claims office of United Risks Mutual Insurance Company. The claims department took up the entire ground floor of a brick-faced modern office building, its darkened windows placed at equal intervals. He entered the lobby and waited ten minutes for claims representative Harlan Getz to appear. The young receptionist was pleasant enough and offered him a coffee while he waited. He declined and settled into a cushy chair. *No, I want a lot more from this place than* *a cup of coffee*, he mused, faking a smile back at the attractive young woman.

"Bruce Harrison?" an expectant Harlan Getz inquired. He was playing his part perfectly.

"Yes, how do you do?" said Bruce, rising and responding in kind to Getz's extended hand.

"Please come this way. So good of you to come in today." As they entered the main claims office, Getz continued his spiel, making sure it was overheard by his teammates. "Mr. Harrison, I've been working on your claim and I finally have authorization to make a reasonable offer to settle it. Let's use the conference room." Getz guided Bruce through the muddle of desks manned by claims representatives on the phones and at their computers. The stale office air mixed with the odor of computer motherboards and reams of paper—all tainted with the whiff of human activity.

About halfway there, he leaned closer to Bruce—his placid face belying the anxiety he felt—and whispered through gritted teeth, "What the hell are you doing here?" The pair settled into the conference room with its lengthy metal and faux wood table and matching chairs. The large window looked out on the rows and rows of desks staffed by Harlan's co-workers.

When the five o'clock buzzer sounded, the two had been "negotiating" in the conference room for half an hour. They were seen but unheard by the claims staff. The insurance company's employees cleared out, leaving them alone and able to talk freely. Once emptied, the cavernous claims office seemed tired and worn from the day's activities.

Harlan, pacing back and forth nervously, was at the point of whining, "Bruce, or whatever your name is today, I'm done with it. The auditors will be here Friday and are sure to catch onto us." Clearly agitated and waving his arms around, Harlan led Bruce out of the conference room and down a hallway as he ranted on, but in a forced whisper. "You must understand, they look for patterns; especially on amounts over five thousand." Shaking his head, he continued, "I just can't take the pressure anymore." He spun around to face Bruce. "And why would you come into the office today and have everyone get a look at you? Your recklessness is scaring me. These people are not fools. Someone will remember you and put two and two together."

Exasperated, Bruce pushed the smaller Harlan into a corner near a set of stairs leading to the building's basement and shot back, "Listen, you little paper-pushing twit, we started this together and I'm not nearly finished. This has been a cash cow all along. We've gotten away with tens of thousands of dollars and I ain't about to walk away from it." He paused a moment, eyes scanning the large room. Softening his approach, he tried reasoning with Harlan. "You know how to hide those phony files until the snoops are gone. I know you can do it. So... what's the problem?"

"I just can't do it anymore. I'm done!" His head down and right elbow raised, Harlan tried pushing past the stockier man, but when Bruce instinctively shoved back, Harlan lost his balance and fell to his left. With a startled cry, and grasping for anything—but only grabbing air—he tumbled headlong down the stairs.

"Whoa... Look out!" Bruce ran down the stairs after Harlan and found him unresponsive, lying on his left side. Bruce slowed as he reached the bottom. "Jesus! Are you all right?" A weak rasping sound came from the crumpled man's throat. His eyes were half shut and fluttering.

He shook Harlan... nothing. Bruce rolled the smaller man over onto his back and saw that Harlan's neck flopped around uncontrollably. Frustrated, he said aloud, "You broke your neck, you idiot! Now what am *I* supposed to do?"

A frightful thought intensified: *What do I do now?* A rhetorical question, indeed. *I can leave him here to be found... dead or alive by that time.* Beginning to better appreciate his predicament, a chilling certainty gripped Bruce: the stark prospect of going back behind bars. Or *I can finish you off and get out of here without a hitch.* Taking another look at Getz, he lamented, "Sorry, little buddy, this way you won't be able to come clean and implicate me." With that, Bruce grimly grabbed Harlan's head with both hands. He yanked and twisted multiple times as far as he could in both directions, feeling—and hearing—the sickening cracking of cervical vertebrae. Completing his odious task, and with the sensation of Harlan's skin and hair lingering, he wiped his hands on his sides. He sat back on a step and watched. *Fascinating*, he thought. Absent any emotion, he calmly waited. In less than a minute, Harlan's labored breathing slowed, then stopped... life's spark extinguished.

Bruce waited another minute to be sure Getz was dead, then slowly ascended the basement stairs. He headed for the nearest exit while solemnly considering his situation: *Looks like I've graduated from petty thief and scam artist to murderer.* His thoughts flashed over the past year, pondering the obvious: *How could anyone connect me to our slick little scam... or for that matter, tie me to what had just happened at the foot of the stairs? This boy is not going behind bars again for that egotistical little prick!*

It all started when Bruce put in his first of many fraudulent insurance claims. He went to a local cemetery and came up with suitable names and dates of births, then sent away to NoveltyID. com and paid for fake New Jersey driver's licenses. It was so easy. He set up phony addresses in Mailboxes USA and UPS Stores, and sat back satisfied that he had enough false identification to make his scam work.

Bruce then performed his "fake fall-down gig," as he called it, in supermarkets, office buildings, and apartment complexes. He even used mild disguises, such as dark-rimmed glasses, a stick-on moustache, and slick-backed hair. While not completely changing his appearance, it was enough to fool just about anyone who might try to connect the claims and attribute them to one person—him.

The doctors he visited sent him to physical therapists, and the claim was constructed and expanded. Everything changed, however, when claims representative Harlan Getz of United Risks Mutual Insurance Company caught onto the scheme—and wanted in. Bruce was not wild about the idea of a partnership, but, he thought, *It's not like I have a choice in the matter.*

At first, Harlan was enthusiastic. "Oh man, this is great! I know this system inside and out. I know what looks good in the claim file and what I can get away with. You just leave it to me," he told Bruce. "What you have been doing up to now is peanuts compared to what we can do together—and with much less risk. I've been dreaming of having someone on the outside, and here you are," he declared. "By the way, knock it off with the other companies. You've been lucky up to now; some of them audit all the time."

Harlan continued with the warning, "To really get away with this, though, I'll have to occasionally put the brakes on by 'nego- tiating' a good deal for the company. In other words, Brucey, we ain't gonna kill the goose that laid the golden egg."

Brucey? He calls me that again and I'll…

So began this criminal collaboration between two opposites, their personalities such that they barely tolerated each other. Yet for both, it was just a matter of business. Harlan would see that Bruce's claims were routed to him with their various fake names and addresses. Then he would put memos into the file supporting his contacts with the "non-attorney" represented, so-called "controlled claimants," creating a plausible flow that his supervisors would see as normal activity. When the time was right, and the file built up enough, Harlan would settle the fraudulent claim with one of his "Bruces," and an insurance check would be cut. The checks were deposited in bank accounts that Bruce set up in three different New Jersey counties. He had sufficient identification to open accounts and even write checks back and forth between accounts—again, on Harlan's advice. Bruce had to hand it to Harlan. *He may be an arrogant little geek, but he sure knows how to pull this off. My ace-in-the-hole is he doesn't know who I really am... just good ole "Bruce." Sweet!*

Bruce followed Harlan's plan on the outside to a T. He would visit certain doctors chosen by Harlan and provide the physical complaints the doctors would fall for. At one point, Bruce had eleven claims going at once. He had to keep notes just to keep it all straight. Harlan had him submitting lost wages, using phony letterheads for companies that didn't exist. He even slid relabeled x-rays lifted from closed claim files in the insurance company's basement into those phony files.

He knew that once a claim was settled, it rarely was revisited. He also knew that the bosses—especially the claims manager—were interested only in how many claims were settled in a month. They were judged on their closures, nothing else; hence, they looked past any patterns out of the ordinary. Anything that Harlan's fertile mind could think of to give their scam the appearance of legitimacy was employed. In fact, it became a game for him—his way of putting one over on the system he hated. *I'll show 'em*, thought Harlan. *They think they know it all and can't be beaten. They are so wrong!*

Harlan's hubris came to an end, however, when a claims adjuster in the New Brunswick office was caught working his own fraudulent claim. The company responded quickly and harshly. The internal auditors did an exhaustive review of that adjuster's files. Harlan was truly impressed with the way the auditors did their job and the example made of that New Brunswick adjuster, who not only lost his job, but was arrested. After that, Harlan lost his nerve. So, when Bruce appeared at the office unexpectedly on Monday afternoon, Harlan flipped out.

The little jerk, Bruce thought, as he pictured Harlan's body at the foot of the stairs. *Now he's dead and not only has my cash flow stopped, but there could also be an investigation.* He was reminded of Harlan's admonition: "*Someone will remember you and put two and two together.*" That made him uneasy as well.

As Bruce threw open the side door leading to the alley and parking lot next to the United Risks building, he pulled out the cotton padding from inside his cheeks and peeled off the thin moustache. No longer in disguise, he suddenly bumped face-first into a woman walking rapidly along the alley next to the building. They both froze momentarily, stepped back, excused themselves, and continued on. Bruce glanced over his shoulder. *She's really looking back at me. Why is she looking back?*

CHAPTER
Two

Nothing is so burdensome as a secret.

French proverb

Monday, 5:15 p.m.

he stared at the ceiling, tears welling up and over-flowing, trickling their way along her cheeks and puddling in her ears. She turned her head on the pillow to look out of the window. The leaves were just starting to turn now in late August. Melancholy overwhelmed her. She heard the traffic in the distance and wondered how many of those people were having extramarital affairs, too. The bed suddenly felt foreign and cold. She got up and with a newfound sense of modesty, faced away from her bed partner and dressed. "It's over, Johnny."

"What are you talking about? Haven't we had a good time?" said her young lover, now up on one elbow. "What do you think Boyd is up to right now? You deserve better, Callie."

"I just can't keep up this charade, Johnny Boy. Two wrongs don't... you know. I feel terribly guilty, and besides, everywhere I go I imagine private detectives are following me." When she finished dressing, she went over to the bed and placed her hand on Johnny's cheek. "You are a sweet boy and if things were different... but they're not, are they?"

Johnny reached for her hand, but she pulled away and headed for the door of the small apartment. "Goodbye, Johnny. It *was* nice, but it's over."

Callie Brooks Richards, at forty-two, was a tall, thin, attractive blonde; the only daughter of Gordon Cecil Brooks, III, a wealthy Wall Street magnate. Her carefree days of partying and haphazard dating ended when she met Boyd Richards. She was fresh out of college, he just out of law school. Boyd was everything she ever wanted: educated, good looking, attentive, and on his way up. It took another ten years, but his law office took off with no small help from Callie's father. Now, twenty years later, Boyd's firm was getting ready for another young associate to be added to his staff of seven lawyers and the usual retinue of paralegals and secretaries. Interviews were under way.

It was also helpful that his father-in-law funded Boyd's political ambitions. When he ran for office in the 7th Congressional

District of New Jersey, Callie stood by his side throughout the knock-down, drag-out campaign. In a close contest, Boyd lost to James Barnett, a war hero, who had the inside track with the strong New Jersey Democratic Party. Nevertheless, that campaign put the public spotlight on Boyd, leaving no doubt he would inevitably return to the political arena. Callie and Boyd became regulars at political rallies and social functions throughout Central New Jersey. They joined Trump National Golf Club in Bedminster and reveled in the attention that came with membership in upper society. Their photographs—she with her blonde hair wrapped in a stylish French twist, he in his tuxedo with that full head of steely gray hair—appeared in local newspapers with other socialites, always impeccably dressed and smiling that "We have made it" look for the camera.

Callie understood financially successful men had inflated egos, and she did her best to see that her man was happy. But when the twins, Amy and Josh, left the nest and went off to college, things changed. Boyd seemed distracted and distant. With the kids gone, finding conversation of mutual interest was awkward. His seeming indifference made her wonder if Boyd was having an affair. He made excuses for coming home late and even went off to work on the weekends, which was unusual. She reasoned, *He has people for that.* She tried to shake those thoughts, but then the subject came up again.

Three months ago, she and her tennis pal, Grace Harjes, were sitting courtside sipping on ice teas when Grace said, "Callie, I am worried about you."

"What do you mean?"

"You and Boyd have been together... how long is it now?"

"Twenty years, Gracie. I cannot believe it, myself," Callie said, tilting her head stoically.

"Well, you know these guys get itchy around the twenty mark. Something about their manhood clock ticking. My Dennis went through it," Gracie said with a wistful look. "You never know."

"Are you trying to tell me something?"

"Not for me to say, my friend, but you might want to boost up your radar."

"You *are* trying to tell me something—out with it!"

"Okay, but don't shoot the messenger, sweetie. We have been friends for too long. It's just that guys and their locker room talk doesn't always stay there, if you know what I mean. Dennis came home from their golf game last weekend with a sly smile on this face. I asked him 'Hey, D-man, what's with the Cheshire Cat face?' and all he could say was, 'That Boyd... he's got a secret. A pretty one, I think.'"

"Oh, please, Grace. Like you said, guys talk and try to impress each other. Not Boyd, no way," said Callie, putting on her strongest denial face, waiving off the very idea.

"Okay, dearie. I'm just saying, stay alert. Gotta go now. Say good night, Gracie."

"Good night, Gracie."

Callie was on her guard after that and her fears were boosted when phone calls came to the house with no one answering at the other end. She mentioned it to Boyd, but he blew it off, saying, "Probably friends of the kids messing around." Callie's concern grew.

When she and Grace next played tennis, the subject came up again. "Grace, you were right. Boyd is having an affair. I just feel it."

Sweetie, when D-man pulled that, I fixed him. I had a fling of my own. It worked. We went through our counseling and came out the other end better off than before. But it was the tit-for-tat that brought him around."

"I couldn't do that, Grace."

"Sure, you can. Wait!" Grace exclaimed, half-standing up and waving, "Johnny Boy, come over here. There's someone I'd like you to meet." That's how it started with Callie and the twenty-five-year-old tennis pro.

Now, as Callie left him in his small loft apartment, she felt a mixture of guilt and relief. She would get it straight with Boyd, and they would sign up for counseling, too. But she could never let him know of her own dalliance. Never!

Callie was reflective as she walked. *I'm glad I parked in that insurance company parking lot. Going through this alley is a good way of seeing if I'm being followed. Johnny's idea.*

"What the… Oh, I'm so sorry!" She bumped into a man hurriedly coming out the side door of the insurance building. He was just as startled as she. For a moment they both stared at each other. Gaining her composure, she continued on toward her parked car. She looked back intently and wondered, *Could he be a private investigator? Maybe. He's really looking at me.*

CHAPTER
Three

Certain signs precede certain events.
Cicero – Roman politician

Tuesday, 8:05 a.m.

e had been sitting in the rental van for an hour, intending to stay all day, if necessary. He got there before the insurance company opened and parked the white Dodge rental van in the adjoining parking lot amidst other similar vehicles. At 8:45 a.m. the action started. The first police car arrived, followed by an EMT crew in an ambulance and another patrol car. Clearly, someone had discovered Harlan's body at the bottom of the stairs upon opening for business. Bruce was interested in the official reaction the discovery caused. He was sure he would be able to tell if it would be treated as an accident or a homicide.

By noon, there had been no plainclothes vehicles. The medical examiner's van arrived, but stayed only half an hour. Bruce watched the medical examiner's grunts heft the lumpy body bag into the van and then drive off. *So far, so good*, he thought. *No detectives, no forensics. Perfect. I'll give it one more day here. In the meantime, I have a date with a pretty lady.*

Tuesday, 12:35 p.m.

Yesterday, right after their accidental encounter in the alley, Bruce was able to get to his van in time to follow the woman to her home just three miles away. He could not take a chance that the woman he bumped into at the insurance company's side door might identity him at some later date should the Getz death be ruled a homicide. Cruising around Summit's Manor Hill environs, he thought: *This is a fancy neighborhood. I bet everyone around here pays close attention to strange cars poking around. I'll have to be careful. I'll come up with something for tomorrow.*

Now, while driving along the adjoining block, the problem resolved itself. He couldn't believe his luck. An empty house backing up to the women's backyard fit his need and its lush vegetation provided concealment. He hunkered down and waited, thinking, *She's home alone on a sunny day with a pool in the backyard. She'll probably come out if I'm patient.* After the better part of an hour, she emerged from the rear of the home through a set of French doors and lowered herself into a lounge chair with her back to him—just twenty-five or so feet away. The woman put in her earbuds, tapped her finger a few times on her smart phone and wriggled deeper into the chair, allowing herself a deep sigh. Bruce chuckled, surprised at his own aplomb, considering what he knew was coming. He silently moved out into the open, covering the distance in seconds. A twisted thought materialized: *This is your captain speaking. Please remain seated, as we anticipate some turbulence ahead.*

CHAPTER
Four

The eternal quest of the individual
human being is to shatter his loneliness.
Norman Cousins – American journalist

Claude Frederick "Mack" Mackey was six months short of his fiftieth birthday. At an even six feet tall with a trim figure and straight-up posture, he would give a younger appearance were it not for the bald spot separating a rim of graying hair, which he kept very short. Mack spent a decade in law enforcement before opening his private investigation agency shortly after the death of his beloved Margaret. He has since harbored guilt for not being there when, racked by cancer, she died alone at home just ten years into their time together. Childless, he and Margaret did everything together. They were fast friends before love dawned on them. They were married in the chapel of Plainfield's First Presbyterian Church on Watchung Avenue, just down the street from city hall — the same city hall where Mack took his oath of office as a patrolman in those early years.

Mack did well on the Plainfield Police Department and was assigned to the detective bureau within five years—not an easy accomplishment. After a few years, he had the opportunity to move up to the Union County Prosecutor's Office in Elizabeth, New Jersey, so he took it. There, at the county level, he witnessed politics at its worst. He saw decisions made that accommodated political ends rather than better serving the public, and it sickened him. The final straw was when he was ordered to look the other way during a gambling raid. The county sheriff's brother was among those rounded up that day; yet Mack never saw his name on a booking card.

His decision to leave the job was a tough one, because he enjoyed the interaction with the public, as well as with his fellow detectives. But he had become disillusioned and believed time was running out. He knew he could do better in the private sector. His friend and co-worker, Bill Worten, tried to dissuade Mack, but the latter's mind was made up. "You stay here, Bill, and wade through the muck; it's not for me, anymore!"

He had to admit that Margie's death added to his cynicism, which helped along his decision to leave law enforcement. More than anything else, however, it was her death that put Mack into a depression he couldn't seem to shake. Everywhere he went and whatever he did reminded him of their times together. He sold the house and moved into a condo in North Plainfield overlooking

Route 22. It was convenient to his office and offered the solitude he needed. Mack was no dummy. He knew he was miring in his own misery and that it wasn't healthy; but he just couldn't come to grips with life without his soulmate. Then one day change knocked on his door, so to speak.

The Mets are up by three, but that's happened before, then they blow it, he thought. *I wonder what's on the news?* He was reaching for the clicker when he heard a commotion outside in the hallway. It was more like a scuffle: loud voices and one of them was that of a woman who was crying.

"What's goin' on here?" Mack demanded.

A man in a leather jacket turned away from the woman he had pinned against the concrete wall and, pointing a threatening finger at Mack, said, "Hey! You mind your own goddamn business, Jack!" The woman had her arms up defensively and was bleeding from her forehead.

Mack's response was instantaneous. Ignoring the man's warning, he lunged forward and grabbed that extended index finger with his right hand and bent it backward until it snapped. At the same time, he pulled the man forward and landed a solid kick just below the left kneecap. Mack spun him around and slammed the guy into the wall.

"It's Mack, not Jack. Nice to meet you, too." Mack moved in closer, shoving the other man's chest a couple of times exercising control. "You beat it out of here right now, Buster, before I add to your hurt. Got it?"

Wide-eyed and in obvious pain, "Buster" nodded quickly and went limp. Mack added a couple more chest percussions, then pulled the guy away from the wall and shoved him toward the stairs. Just before descending, the man turned around to say something, but Mack threw him a hard look, put a finger to his pursed lips and shushed him. The guy got the message and left holding his injured hand to his midsection.

Mack turned to the woman. She was still huddled against the wall. Blood trickled down her face and mingled with her tears. She was a mess. Mack touched her shoulder and she recoiled. "It's okay. It's okay. Let me take a look at that," indicating her forehead.

"No, I'm all right. I'll be all right."

"No, you won't. Come with me." Mack firmly steered her shoulders through his still-open condo door and sat her down at the kitchen table.

"Really," she faked a brave smile. "You don't have to do anything."

Ignoring her protest, Mack put two Aleves and a glass of water in front of her. "You'll need these," he said while assessing her forehead. "You're gonna have a bump there, for sure." Returning from the bathroom half a minute later, he said, "Don't think you'll need stitches." He blotted the deep scrape with a cotton ball and alcohol. She barley flinched. Mack, paying close attention to her forehead, asked, "Boyfriend?"

"Ex-husband... jerk, womanizer, gambler, and all-around loser. Um, thanks for..."

He interrupted with his hand out, "Nah, none needed. I'm Mack."

"So I heard, and very persuasively," she shook his hand, laughing. He liked her laugh.

"I'm Penny," she said, and with a jerk of her head toward his door, she added, "three doors down that-a-way. Noting his wedding ring, she asked, "And where is Mrs. Dragon Slayer?"

Mack blinked several times. "Lost her to cancer, a couple of years ago."

After an awkward couple of seconds, Penny rose and said, "Sorry. Uh, gotta go." As she neared the doorway, she glanced back with a hand-on-hip pose, saying, "Hmmph... a tough guy with gentle hands—that's a new one on me!"

After she'd gone, Mack cleared the mess on the kitchen table and allowed a wistful thought: *How 'bout that?* He smiled. Somehow, the Mets game was no longer the imperative it had been earlier.

CHAPTER
Five

Deliberation is the work of many men. Action, of one alone.
Charles de Gaulle – Former president of France

Tuesday, 4:36 p.m.

ike many suburban cities and towns in New Jersey, Summit is a mostly friendly residential and family-oriented community. Because of its clean mountain air and easy reach to New York City, Summit attracted the very wealthy in the waning days of the nineteenth century. Those large summer estates, together with mansions built by new money, are now part of a more modern lifestyle. Yet some second and third generations of the old guard still inhabited the neighborhoods. The tree-lined streets and hilly terrain make for a bucolic atmosphere. Just taking a slow drive through its neighborhoods transports one to a simpler time, before the push-and-shove of today. This is also a community unaccustomed to crime—specifically, murder.

The four-thousand-square-foot colonial home in the high-priced Manor Hill section of Summit was a hubbub of activity—just not the kind its neighbors were used to. Several local police cars with their flashing red and blue emergency lights silently ramped up the excitement. Other unmarked vehicles, obviously detective sedans, were parked hodgepodge in the driveway and on the street in front. One parked vehicle was less subtle with its markings: "Union County Medical Examiner." That van's presence suggested death within the home—likely of the unnatural variety.

Unemotional police radio chatter could be heard by murmuring neighbors assembled at a respectful distance, yet close enough to satisfy their curiosity. One neighbor, however, was much closer to the action. She was standing next to one of the police cruisers with its driver door still open from the hurried arrival of the first responding officer.

"How do you spell that again, Grace," asked the young detective patiently.

"H-A-R-J-E-S," she replied. "God, I cannot believe it. Callie was my best friend in the world." Grace had her arms protectively folded across her breasts. She rocked back and forth as she answered the many questions being put to her. Grace Harjes, tennis partner and friend of Callie Richards, discovered her friend's body an hour ago.

"I crossed from my house to the Richards's when Callie wouldn't answer her cell phone. I thought, 'She's probably got those damned earphones in listening to one of those smutty stories again.' When there was no answer at the front door, I walked along the stepping stones on the side of the house, through the garden, and to the pool area. Then I saw her..." Grace's voice trailed off.

That's when Grace came upon the grizzly scene. The body was splayed out face-up next to the pool behind the house. Callie's stillness and glaze-eyed expression told a shaken Grace all she needed to know: Callie was dead. But it was the large pool of blood that had collected on the concrete and the many stab marks clearly defined on Callie's white blouse that hit Grace like a sledgehammer. In the first several seconds Grace couldn't process the scene mentally. She stiffened and held her breath for a second, then screamed repeatedly, as she ran back to her house to call 911.

"So much blood, I can't believe it! Who could do such a thing?" she asked the detective. Her sobbing between answers made it difficult for the detective, who was trying to get as much detail as possible. Experience taught him that initial interviews often produced important evidence at murder scenes, so he persevered.

"Have you and the victim been friends a long time?" he asked, and then went through the litany of inquiry intended to bring him and other investigators up to speed as to relationships and habits—and maybe even offer a possible motive. When the questioning got around to asking about possible trouble in the Richards's marriage, Grace recoiled angrily, "Absolutely not!" Her voice an octave higher now. "They were a loving couple, and I resent the implication." But the question brought back her courtside discussions with Callie and an uneasiness settled over her. "I'm sorry, but I have to go home. I think I'm gonna be sick."

Meanwhile, at poolside the medical examiner was doing his preliminary look-see. Dr. Jacob Restin, having been at it for many years, was used to poking and pinching dead bodies. He had the habit of talking to them while doing so, as well, "So, pretty lady. What are you going to tell me about your attacker? Was he tall or short, left- or right-handed, methodical or in a rage? We'll see, won't we?" He rolled the victim up on one side to look underneath, then gently let her back down.

"Okay, Doc, here's what I see as obvious," said the chief of county detectives, Bill Worten. "I see multiple stab wounds and no evidence of fighting back. Nothing under the nails and no other visible bruises or defensive cuts. Looks like a sudden, surprise attack, maybe coming from behind. How am I doing?"

"Show off. You're probably right. It doesn't seem there was a struggle. Maybe a quick, deliberate attack. I'll know more after the autopsy, but I do notice something. Don't know if it means anything yet."

"C'mon, Doc, give!"

"Well, you see this largest entry wound just below the sternum, where the blood seems to have gushed out more than the others? I think this may have been the first strike and from behind, like you say, but from overhead. You see where the sharp edge of the knife—assuming for now that it was a knife—is on the upper edge of the wound and the wider part is below? Also, the slice mark is almost completely vertical. She might have been sitting in that chair over there and the killer came up and stabbed her from behind and above. The other twelve or so entry wounds seem to be from the same knife, but look shallow; kind of tentative. I will, of course, have to do some dissecting to confirm all this, but that's how I see it for now. I'm just speculating, but a long enough knife at the site of that larger wound—and at the right angle—could have easily sliced her aorta bringing about almost immediate death. That's a really quick bleed-out!"

"Makes sense, Doc. And the phone and earbuds over here gave the perp the advantage of stealth. The chair is tipped over in this direction, and that there's no blood on it doesn't matter. As soon as she was hit with the first blow, she would have reacted by pushing up and away, which is why she landed here. The perp probably then came over to her and continued the attack while she was on the ground."

"Yeah, see how the other entry wounds all seem to come from her left side and are on a horizontal plane to her feet? He probably got down on one knee for that. But, Bill, those shallow and tentative wounds don't make sense right now. We'll see."

"How about time of death, Doc?"

"Let's see, her joints are flexible. The eyelids have lost tension, and the lower jaw has fallen a little bit. Yet, her muscles have not fully stiffened. I would say between four and six hours ago this lady was a beautiful living human being."

After the scene was photographed, videoed and everything dusted for fingerprints, the body was wrapped in a zippered black bag and taken out to the M.E.'s van.

Chief Worten's cell phone buzzed. It was his boss, Union County Prosecutor Raymond Lant, saying he was on the way. Worten briefed him on what he knew and hung up. "See ya at the morgue, Doc. The prosecutor will be here soon."

"Good luck with that!" said Doc Restin with raised eyebrows, as he followed Callie's bag to the front of the house.

County Detective Al Gilhooley was done interviewing Grace Harjes for the time being, so he appeared poolside with Worten. "Do you know who this victim is, boss?"

"Yeah, Mrs. Boyd Richards. Socialite. Wife of a big-shot local politician. And a whole bunch of pressure on us! By the way, the eighth floor is on his way, so you'd better get busy out front and see if you can dig up anyone who knows anything more about this family."

Worten brooded. *Why do the politicians have to show up and not only tread all over my crime scene, but also invariably give the press too much information?* In fact, the press had already arrived out front. The CBS and NBC field trucks were extending their overhead communication dishes, careful to avoid power lines in the process. This would make the New York evening news, and aggressive reporters were already on the scene banging on doors and interviewing anyone in the neighborhood willing to talk on camera.

"Chief Worten?" came the call from the front of the house. Worten, recognizing the prosecutor's voice, fretted... *and the circus begins!* "Back here, Raymond."

Prosecutor Raymond Lant, a tall, gaunt and impeccably dressed African American, walked out of the garden with his usual loping gait. Trailing him closely was another tall man with graying hair wearing a suit Worten thought probably cost more than his own monthly salary. The man was agitated and looking around wildly. Worten recognized him immediately as the victim's husband. "Mr. Richards, you should not be here. I am truly sorry for your loss, but it isn't proper for you to be anywhere near here at this moment."

"This is my home!" Richards replied indignantly. "I have to learn from Raymond here that my wife has been murdered, and you have the nerve to tell me where I should or shouldn't be?" The man was shaking. Dried tears on his cheeks told Worten that Richards had passed through the first shock of his loss and was now lashing out in anger. Acceptance had not yet arrived. Worten's next thought was, *This doesn't look like acting; but I've been fooled before."*

"Chief Worten, Boyd here is a lawyer and a personal friend of mine," said the prosecutor. "I want him kept in the loop at all times, understand?" Boyd Richards was wandering over toward the pool of blood left behind by the M.E.'s crew.

"Sir, all due respect, but you know I cannot do that." Worten turned in the direction of the other man. "Mr. Richards, you can't go over there. This is still a crime scene." Throwing an impatient look back at the prosecutor, he added, "Correction: *my* crime scene."

Sensing an unneeded showdown, the prosecutor turned to his companion, "You know, Boyd, there's nothing we can do here. Maybe we should meet the twins at the airport and get them settled. They need you right now." He looked up at the magnificent manor house, then back down at the pooled blood. His voice, quieting, "They certainly can't stay here."

Turning back, the prosecutor commanded officiously, "My office, first thing in the morning, Bill!"

CHAPTER
Six

The study of crime begins with the knowledge of oneself.

Henry Miller – Controversial American writer

Wednesday, 8:15 p.m.

Bruce was exhilarated! Reliving the events of the past two days had him charged up. He had no idea killing another human could be so... *What's the word? Stimulating. Yes, that's it.* He had crossed a forbidden line into a new world, and there was no turning back. He had done it, and that was that; but he was a little surprised at his own cool detachment toward both Getz and the blonde woman. He rationalized, *It was too bad they had to die, but there was no way he could be arrested and end up in jail for insurance fraud.* His own experience with jail flooded back to him and hardened his resolve: *No, I did the right thing. I will never in my life go into a jail again. Never!*

Following his discharge from the U.S. Army two years ago, Bruce submitted applications to all the local police departments. Since he had been trained and served three years as a military policeman, it seemed a natural progression to switch over to civilian law enforcement. He kept himself in shape with jogging and pushups. He even paid his own way through the Union County Police Academy to become a certified law enforcement officer, a requirement for the hiring of police recruits. Ultimately, he was accepted as a corrections officer stationed in Rahway State Prison. It wasn't the job he was looking for, but it would do until the right one came up. He went through the preliminary correction classes and excelled on the tests. At first, he followed an experienced officer through the various cell blocks, then he was assigned to work night shifts on his own. This was a normal path for rookies.

It was during these solitary night tours that Bruce received his real indoctrination. He was experiencing correctional living first-hand and seeing bad things—things those on the outside could scarcely imagine. His discussions with prisoners of all stripes and his observations of prison life had a profound impact on him: the agony of loneliness, the pecking order among inmates and just being locked up with them was unnerving. The loud clanging of the sliding admission gate behind him when he reported for work each night made his neck stiffen each time he heard it. But most of all, it was the terrible screams of the powerless being violated in the dark that gave him chills. "C.O., help me... *please!*" But he couldn't. It was beyond his capability to interfere with inmate "relations." It was an unwritten rule. It was life behind bars.

Those screams were never far away. In his terrible dream, Bruce's horror was aroused time after time: *I am locked in a cell with two inmates. They are reaching out for me. Oh God! No!* He would jerk to a half-awakened restlessness, his sweat-soaked pillow attesting to his torment. He would get out of bed and do pushups until he could no longer dislodge himself from the floor—his muscles utterly depleted. Pushups were his way of warding off the dark side. Pushups: fighting exhaustion with exhaustion. Pushups: an escape from those lurking evils, as endorphins massed together to block those images. Pushups: his way of surviving those long-ago days locked in the closet, then, as a nine-year-old with echoes of his mother's many beatings permeating his immature mind. *Pushups: my friends, my protectors!*

Bruce was counseled by the prison psychiatrist in hopes of somehow overcoming his anxiety, but it was not to be. Ultimately, he resigned, citing "incompatibility with the demands of the job."

Time spent at Rahway State Prison was not an entire waste. Bruce's conversations with prisoners during the long nights not only made the time go faster, but also contributed to his "education" in another way. Those con men and fraudsters stoically serving out their sentences were happy to have a cordial relationship with a C.O. and opened up to him—mostly bragging about how they pulled off their scams. Integrating that "street experience" with what he learned about fraud and identity theft in the police academy inspired Bruce. An entrepreneurial state of mind crept in. Thus, his sojourn into generating fraudulent insurance claims began. While antithetical to law enforcement, where his first hopes rested, he rationalized his chosen path. *Gotta make a living somehow.* But now his crimes had escalated dramatically. Two killings. *Guess I'm not the guy I thought I was.*

Bruce grabbed the remote and began surfing the television channels. He stopped when CBS News was in the middle of reporting a murder in a wealthy section of Summit. He had to switch to NBC to get the whole story from beginning to end. The screen showed the front of the Richards home as the young reporter submitted her story to viewers. "I am standing in front of the Boyd and Callie Richards home in an exclusive section of Summit, New Jersey. We are not allowed access to the crime scene in the backyard; but that is where Callie Richards, wife of unsuccessful congressional candidate Boyd Richards, was murdered in cold blood. Sources tell NBC News that she was stabbed to death back there. At the moment, police are holding back information, as their investigation proceeds. This is a case we will be following. Back to you in the studio, Tom."

Bruce smiled and thought, *Wow. A big-shot politician.* Then, second thoughts: *There will be a lot of investigation into this one. I better stay on top of this, myself.*

Following his usual rigorous pushup routine, Bruce got up and stepped out onto the small porch attached to his trailer on Springfield Avenue, just off Interstate 78 in Union, New Jersey. There were times when the confining nature of the trailer closed in on him. It reminded him of his night shifts at the prison. Indeed, the claustrophobic closet of his youth slinked in from time to time, as well. He couldn't afford to buy a house or even rent an apartment without a legal source of income. For the time being, he would be content living in the trailer his mother left him when she died last year. He reminisced about his return from the Army and sitting here with his alcoholic mother. His abusive father left many years ago when Bruce grew big enough and strong enough at seventeen to break the old man's nose during one of their many domestic battles.

Bruce resolved with gritted teeth and hatefully narrowed eyes, *That's all in the past. I am my own man now. Nothing and no one is going to stand in my way. I will do whatever it takes to survive!*

CHAPTER
Seven

A politician... one that would circumvent God.

**William Shakespeare, Hamlet – English poet
and playwright**

Thursday, 9:30 a.m.

*R*aymond Lant enjoyed his position as prosecutor**. He was the first African American in the
history of New Jersey to be appointed as a county's chief law
enforcement officer. While he hated the politics, he was a prag-
matist. He would say to his wife, Veronica, "I'm just a simple
guy swimming with the sharks." She would reply, "Just be sure
you come home with all your appendages!"

In fact, he had a shark waiting in his outer office right now.
"Come in, Sheila. Please, sit!" Sheila Cummings was as ambi-
tious as they come. The youngest daughter of a single mother,

she had three siblings. Sheila grew up knowing how to fend for herself. She worked her way through Rutgers University in New Brunswick by waiting tables. Once admitted to Rutgers Law School, she had to attend most of her classes in Newark. She lucked out with a job in an insurance company's claims department, which accommodated her evening law classes. It took longer than most, but she stuck with it, receiving her law degree just before her thirtieth birthday.

Her mature bearing gave her an advantage over others vying for the job in the prosecutor's office, and her internship there during the summer of her senior year of law school didn't hurt either. Sheila was ambivalent when it came to the women's movement, but she didn't hold disdain for any benefits that came her way from that source, either. She had a tough exterior, and she could swear like a sailor if the occasion required it.

"So, Sheila, I gave you this assignment because I know you can handle it." Pulling his chair closer, Prosecutor Lant added, "All I will demand of you is fairness and sticking to the book, understand?"

She nodded, "Of course, Mr. Lant. I will not let you down. How do you want me to get started?"

"Get together with Chief Worten and Detective Gilhooley. They are the principal investigators on the Richards murder case." His voice softening, "I guess you know, Mr. Richards and I are close friends, which is the reason I am recusing myself." Abruptly, he signaled the meeting was over by turning his back to

her, facing his computer, and saying, "I know you will do well."
Prosecutor Lant's ego was still stinging from political pressure
to recuse himself and assign Ms. Cummings.

"Yes, I understand," she replied, as she got up to leave. But
she already had the inside track. The county chairman's phone
call earlier told her of what was to come. He also set up a meeting
for her later in the evening with someone else.

The Pluckemin Inn was the perfect out-of-the-way place for
a secret meeting. Located on Route 206 in Bedminster, it was
far from the prying eyes in the county courthouse environs of
Elizabeth. It was also a classy, upscale setting that wholly suited
another's purpose.

James Barnett, Democratic congressman for the 7th District
of New Jersey, rose and signaled to Sheila when she entered
the restaurant. She dressed carefully for the occasion in a gray
pants suit with her hair pulled back in a small bun. It was her
best business-like look.

"Thank you for coming, Ms. Cummings. I've heard good
things about you." He pulled out the chair for Sheila in a solicitous manner.

"Thank you, Congressman."

"Please call me James."

That's not going to happen. "Sir, I appreciate the praise and
meeting with you, of course; but what is this all about? At my
level, I'm just not used to this kind of attention." Oh, Sheila

knew. She just wanted to limit the unnecessary platitudes. *Let's cut the crap and get down to business*, she thought.

Slowly stirring and staring into his cocktail, Barnett said, "I was told you were blunt, a no-nonsense type. I like that. I guess you know I pulled some strings to get you assigned to the Richards murder case, right?"

Sheila nodded.

"If by any chance your investigation should point to a particular person as the killer of poor Mrs. Richards, I would want to be kept advised of the details." He stopped stirring and looked Sheila straight in the eye. "This is all off the record, Ms. Cummings." He settled back in his chair, "You can have a bright future, if you play ball." Smiling confidently, he went on, "My father used to say, 'If you want to play in the big leagues, you have to know how to swing the bat.' I hope you are getting my drift."

"Congressman Barnett, I have just one thing to say to you."

"What's that?" He squirmed apprehensively, not at all sure of what was coming.

Sheila smiled. Cupping her hands to her mouth, she vocalized, "Play ball!"

Barnett grinned and adjusted his napkin. "The brisket here is the best!'"

CHAPTER
Eight

Trouble will rain on those who are already wet.

Anonymous

Thursday, 11:18 a.m.

*T*he refrigerator atmosphere chilled over him, as Chief Worten pushed open the door to the medical examiner's laboratory. "Okay, Doc, what's the news today?"

"Hey, Bill. How did it go with the prosecutor this morning?"

Worten had a puzzled look on his face. *How did he know I met with Raymond?*

"C'mon, pal. Nothing goes on around here unknown to the underground gossip machine. It's county politics."

"Yeah, I suppose so. Anyway, Raymond recused himself, and Sheila Cummings is now on the case. Because 'Mr. Prosecutor' is too close to the Richards family, he didn't feel he should be involved. Too bad he didn't feel that way yesterday when he showed up at the crime scene with Boyd Richards in tow right after you left. Not that Boyd is a suspect—then again everyone is in the beginning, you know?"

"I can't believe the prosecutor would walk onto a crime scene with the vic's husband. Must've been a temporary lack of judgment, huh?"

Worten, shaking his head, changed the subject. "Raymond didn't want Cummings, but the county chairman gave him no choice. All he wanted to do this morning was to warn me about Sheila and her political ambitions. Once we go down the road on this one, it's gonna be a tightrope act, for sure."

"Better you than me."

"Enough of that, let's get back to your bailiwick, Doc."

"Okay, I'm glad you stopped by, Bill." Dr. Restin, now in his lab coat, got right to the point. "These *were* tentative stab marks on the vic's chest, and I think this looks like an attempt to make it look like a crime of passion." Restin pulled back the sheet covering Callie Richards. "I say this because when an enraged killer starts by stabbing deeply, he doesn't ease up, as his pent-up frenzy plays out, he continues to stab and stab until his anger is sated. In my experience, this was probably done by someone who, by inflicting the other dozen wounds, was trying to make it look like an out-of-control killer as opposed to a calculated attack." The M.E.'s frown deepened and he looked up at Worten. "Bill, if I am right, what you have here is a pretty savvy perp."

"Interesting theory. I'll pass it on to my crew." Worten stepped back, body language suggesting he was done here.

"Don't leave yet, Bill. I have another one for you," Doc Restin said as he motioned the detective over to another body gurney nearby. He pulled back the sheet revealing the pale and lifeless body of Harlan Getz. "This started out as an accidental broken neck, but I think not."

Curiosity now raised, Worten leaned over the body. "How so?"

"As you know, we have to do a post on anyone not under the care of a physician at the time of death. When this guy came in, the officer said the victim fell down the stairs and broke his neck, and assured me it was an accident. At first, I thought so, too— but when I opened his neck and found complete devastation of his cervical vertebrae, I changed my mind. In order to have that kind of damage, this guy would have had to fall down the stairs a dozen times. To go along with that, he was very likely conscious as he fell, because the pinky of his left hand was fractured along with a dislocated wrist. These are just like defensive wounds, Bill. When you fall," Doc gestured down and away, "you reach out to protect yourself. You can't do that if you are unconscious before the fall. So, this guy's neck was grossly and severely damaged *after* his fall."

"I think you are saying he was murdered after falling down the stairs."

"Yes, I am. Someone inflicted a great deal of trauma to his neck after the fall."

"Great... two in one week!"

As he left the M.E.'s lab, Worten punched in a number on his phone and left a voicemail message for the young detective on the Richards case. "Gilhooley, we just caught another possible homicide, according to the M.E. I want you to go to United Risks Mutual Insurance Company at 4530 Central Avenue in New Providence. When you get there, call me."

CHAPTER
Nine

Chance makes our parents, but choice makes our friends.

Jacques Delille – French poet

*W*hen Mack answered the door, she pushed past him and scurried over to the television. She dropped down on the sofa, cheerily announcing, "I love baseball. Who's winning?"

Mack blinked a few times. "Hello, Penny. Please come in. Would you like to watch the game with me?" His tone was friendly with just a dash of sarcasm, as he closed the door and walked over to the fridge. "Care for a drink?"

"Sure. Whatever you're drinking," she smiled.

There's that smile again, he thought. *Well, would you believe it, Mack? She's cute when she's not bleeding and sniffling. Looks*

like she works out, about thirty-five or so—likin' the freckles, too.
What's not to like here?

They watched the game and, between her enthusiastic out-bursts, began learning more about each other. Penny Lund was from Nesquehoning, Pennsylvania, "where they would bring in the street lights at night, if they had street lights." She was an emergency room nurse at Morristown Memorial Hospital. She loved her work, though it did sometimes bring her into contact with the seamier side of life. When Mack told her of his past police experience, she said, "I knew there was something about you. The way you handled Harry and all."

"Harry... the ex-husband?"

"Yup. Emphasis on *ex*. You know, we have something in common, Mack. We seem to associate with the same dirt bags. We both drink Miller Lite, too."

"Do you ever slow down? You make an optimist look forlorn."

"I'm not gonna be the victim anymore, Mack. I want to live life and be happy. What about you? Still in mourning?"

A little taken aback, he replied defensively, "Pretty direct, too, aren't you?"

Undeterred, Penny said, "I seem to recall something from one of my classes: Chaucer said, 'Time and tide wait for no man.' Think about it, Mack."

"There's more to you than meets the eye, isn't there, Penny? Oh, and not what meets the eye is less than..." Blushing, Mack tried to recover from his verbal stumble. "I mean..."

"Leave it alone," she laughed. "I'll take it as a compliment. I can't imagine you meaning it any other way."

After a long pause, she with her head down and he searching for words, Mack said, "Say, Penny, I have an idea. Bob and Brenda Higgins invited me to a picnic at their place in the country this Sunday. Wanna go with me? Bob and I work together. I think you and Brenda would hit it off. What do you think?"

"You mean like a date?"

"I mean like a... picnic." Mack squirmed a little. Their eyes met, her eyebrows insinuating an obvious challenge. He relented. "Okay, a date."

"Sure. I'm in."

That Sunday, they drove north into New Jersey's scenic mountainous region. Unlike the central and eastern areas of the state, where larger populations live in the shadow and under the influence of New York City, the wooded hills and valleys of Hunterdon, Warren and Sussex counties offer expansive views and a sense of tranquility. They drove along in silence, enjoying the countryside, together.

After a while, Mack broke the silence. "You know, Penny, most people from around the country don't really understand our state. I say I'm from New Jersey; they say, 'What exit?'" They both laughed.

"It really is beautiful up here, isn't it?" Penny said serenely.

"Yeah, it is. I can understand why Bob and Brenda chose to settle here."

"What are they like, Mack?"

"Well, Bob is a great kidder—always with the quips. He's a good loyal pal and a hard worker. I believe the term is 'salt of the earth.' And Brenda is one of those people who says what she means and means what she says... no holds barred. What you see is what you get with Brenda. And I like that."

"Sounds like a fun Sunday comin' up."

When they arrived at the Higgins's country place, Bob and Brenda came out to greet them. Penny got out of the Range Rover, outstretched her arms and slowly moved in a circle, loudly proclaiming, "Now, this is really living! The country air, the birds and bees and squirrels in the trees. This is for me!" Mack laughed, "Jeez, Penny, don't hold back!" He introduced her to his friends and once the quick tour was over, the guys sat at the picnic table, while Brenda and Penny went inside.

"She's nice, Mack. Lots of enthusiasm, huh?"

"You can say that again. I can hardly keep up with her. But I've been moping around too long, Bob. No one could replace Margie; but I really like being with Penny. She's funny and real, if you know what I mean. This is very new, and I don't know where it's going, but it will be interesting." Inside, the two women made small talk for a while as Brenda worked on dinner and Penny offered her help. Then Brenda stopped what she was doing and gazed out the kitchen window at Mack and Bob. "You know, Penny, Mack is very dear to us. He's a good man—a man who suffered a great hurt when his wife died. They were close..."

"Brenda, let me interrupt you. You don't have to tell me he's a good man. He's the best. And if you're thinking what I think you're thinking, you can put that think to rest. I would never add to his pain. I like him very much." She blushed a little, then went on, "He and I seem to have hit if off well enough. We'll see where this relationship is going, but you needn't worry about me. I'm on your side when it comes to Mack." She hesitated a moment, then said, "It's about time I made a good decision in my life."

Bob stuck his head through the kitchen door, "Anybody order a mac 'n cheese?"

Brenda looked at Penny, her eyes rolling, "Jerk! Always with the jokes. If Bob fell out of his boat and was drowning in Round Valley Reservoir, his bubbles would make wise-ass remarks as they popped to the surface."

"If... if wishes were horses, beggars would ride. If horse turds were biscuits, they'd eat till they died." Bob was on a roll.

Brenda punched Bob in the shoulder and they all had a good laugh.

A couple of hours later, all four were seated in lawn chairs around a chimenea fire Bob started. Penny looked over at Mack. He, Brenda and Bob were laughing at something they shared in the past. She thought, *He doesn't express his inner feelings easily, but introducing me to his closest friends today is his way of letting me know I've made it through his stand-off exterior. I think I'm beginning to understand: Pay attention, Penny, and it could work out!*

Her wandering interrupted, she replied, "Huh? Oh, I was just lost in the flames. Sorry, Brenda, what did you say?"

CHAPTER

Ten

A successful lawsuit is the one worn by a policeman.

Robert Frost - American poet

Thursday, 1:38 p.m.

*D*etective Gilhooley, on Worten's instructions, went up to the reception desk in the claims office of United Risks Mutual and asked to speak to the manager. "Tell him I'm here about the guy that was found dead the other day."

Claims manager Charles Howard appeared in the lobby several minutes later and ushered Gilhooley to his office, maneuvering through the sea of desks and the hubbub of work activity in progress. "So how can I help you? It was terrible—a real shock for our people that morning."

"Would you show me where it happened and tell me about the man... Harwood?"

"His name was Harlan. Harlan Getz was one of our long-time adjusters. He was with the company for at least fifteen years and did a good job, overall. Um, tell me, detective, is there a reason you are looking further into this?"

"It's really just routine. Whenever there is an unnatural death, we have to cross all the T's, etcetera. Please show me where he was found, Mr. Howard."

Howard led the detective down the hall to the stairwell where Harlan had breathed his last breath. Taking notes, Gilhooley counted thirteen steps to the bottom and carefully went over every inch of each stair and riser. There were many scuff marks on the walls, as well as on the stairs, but he found nothing attributable to the victim's fall. "Okay, I've seen enough here. Can I speak to some of your staff?" He thought, *At one time, this might have been a crime scene worth processing, but with the delay and people trampling all over it, not anymore.*

Howard arranged for Gilhooley to take over the small conference room located next to the rest rooms. The room was cluttered with claim files stacked on the desk and overflowing onto the floor. The young detective pulled one of the two hard chairs into position for those he would question and slumped down across the desk into the other. With nothing to do for a few minutes, he reached over and opened one of those claim files.

"Let's see," he said aloud, and after a few moments, added, "This doesn't look like the kind of job I would ever do. Too much paperwork." He saw that each claim file had memo after memo to and from the file-handling adjuster setting forth the status of the claim and the adjuster's plan going forward. Clearly, the end game was to close the file by negotiating a satisfactory settlement.

A tentative, "Hello? You wanted to see me?" came through the half-opened door. Once seated, Maria Sanchez just started talking, unprompted by the detective. "Like, I was at my desk just finishing up my monthly report, you know? Alex, the guy on my right, said, 'Maria, check out Getz. There he goes again, like beating up on a claimant. That guy bumps off more controlled claimants than anybody.'"

"What'd he mean by that?" asked Gilhooley.

"Well, Mr. Getz had the rep in the office of being, like, the best negotiator for people who weren't represented by a lawyer. Like, he could talk them into settling like nobody could."

Gilhooley thought a moment, "So, could you hear the conversation between them?"

"Oh, no. But we could see them, like, acting it out. You know? Waving arms, like, pointing at each other, like that. Can I ask a question?"

"Like, what?" Gilhooley couldn't resist.

"Like, why are we doin' all this? He just fell down the stairs, right?"

"It's just that we do this for any serious accident, just in case." That seemed to satisfy Maria, so Gilhooley pressed on, but it became clear Maria had nothing more of importance to share.

Alex, the young man next to Maria, confirmed her observations with an equal number of "likes" and "you knows." Gilhooley made appointments for Maria and Alex to sit down with a police sketch artist, as those two got a good look at the man with Harlan Getz. Gilhooley interviewed six more claims people over the next hour and a half. He learned that Getz was still in the larger-windowed conference room with that unknown man when five o'clock came around and the employees went home. None of those he interviewed knew the identity of the stranger with Getz; but they also surmised he was a controlled claimant being interviewed—not an unusual occurrence. Just to add to the uncertainty, no two descriptions of the man with Getz were even close to one another. *Frustrating, but not all that unusual*, he mused. *Eyewitness testimony: always sketchy and not the best evidence. First thing they taught us in rookie class. But that mystery man was probably the last to see him alive. Gotta be the killer!*

Also Thursday, 1:38 p.m.

From his roost inside the rental van, Bruce perked up when the detective car first pulled up in front of the insurance company. "What's this all about?" he questioned himself. "Maybe just some follow-up for the paperwork." But Bruce was not one for ignoring potential danger. *"Better keep an eye on this place,"* he thought.

Three hours later

Before wrapping up, Gilhooley asked, "Tell me, Mr. Howard, do you have security cameras set up around the outside of the building?"

"Well, yes we do, but..." Howard's painful expression finished the sentence.

"Please, don't tell me. They aren't working?"

"They were, but something happened to the recorder. We have a work order submitted to the regional office for approval."

"I see. Thanks for your cooperation." Gilhooley left the building, walked to his left and entered an alley that ran between the company's parking lot and the next street. As he walked by, he slowed and looked up at the security camera and shook his head. He continued on down the alley and inspected the entire area surrounding the insurance company's building. He noted a residential area on the next block consisting of low- to middle-class houses, but nothing jumped out at him, evidence-wise.

When the detective reappeared and began looking around, Bruce pushed closer to the van window and frowned. *Cameras?*

CHAPTER
Eleven

Truth always lags last, limping along on the arm of time.

Baltasar Gracián – Spanish Jesuit and philosopher

Same day, 4:45 p.m.

etective Gilhooley decided to go back to **Manor Hill Drive** and finish up his interview with Grace Harjes. Her breakdown during the first interview left Gilhooley with the impression she knew more than she was saying. As he walked up to the Harjes front door, he thought, *Best girlfriends know each other's secrets. I have to push Grace a little harder this time.*

"Hello again, Mrs. Harjes. I just have a few more questions for you. May I come in?"

"I really don't…"

"I know you want to help us figure out who killed Callie, right?"

"Yes, but I don't…"

"Oh, I think you do." They stared at each other for a long moment. Gilhooley cocked his head and raised his eyebrows in a persuasive attitude. "You should talk to me, Grace."

Lowering her head, Grace relented and backed up. "Come in."

Grace led the young detective to the family study and directed him to a leather chair. Gilhooley got right to it. "Tell me why you came unglued when I asked about how Callie and Boyd were getting along in their marriage. That's where we left off. And your reaction to my questioning at that point leaves me with more questions. Understand?"

"Callie was a good person." She started to tear up.

"Of course, she was. Why do you continue to say that? No one has said otherwise." Using her first name again, Gilhooley pushed harder. "Grace, whatever is bothering you, it is better if you let it out. We can deal with it."

"It's my fault!" Grace blurted. "I set her up with that Johnny Boy and... Oh, God!"

Gilhooley was able to elicit from Grace all the details leading up to her introduction of Callie to the young tennis pro. As he drove away from Grace's home, he thought, *Now I have motive times two: The husband and the jilted boyfriend.*

He picked up his phone and dialed the office. "Chief, I'm glad I caught ya," Gilhooley said into the phone. "When can we have a meet? I've got a lot of stuff to go over with you on both these cases." Gilhooley hung up and drove back to his office in Elizabeth.

CHAPTER
Twelve

We are never deceived; we deceive ourselves.

Goethe – German writer and statesman

The following Monday, mid-morning

*S*heila **Cummings summoned Chief Bill Worten** and Detective Gilhooley to her eighth-floor office of the Union County Prosecutor's Office. She had just gone over all the reports and had come to the conclusion that she had a viable case against Boyd Richards—albeit, circumstantial.

"Chief Worten, from what I can see, Detective Gilhooley's interview of Grace Harjes leaves little doubt as to who killed the victim in this case. It seems that both might have been having affairs, but, surely, there is no doubt that Callie was. Either way, we have motive for murder, no?"

"I see your point, Ms. Cummings, but we need more before we charge someone like Boyd Richards with cold-blooded murder," said Worten. "We're looking for forensics and maybe more witness testimony. The case is very active. I would advise that we hold off until we have a better case."

"No, I don't see it that way," Sheila shot back. "Why wait? I think his arrest will bring more people forward and—you never know—you might come across the murder weapon or something else, if you keep working it."

"But why take the chance of egg on our faces? The guy isn't going anywhere, right? Let's go by the book and nail the bastard the right way and with a solid case."

Gilhooley chimed in, "Ms. Cummings, I also would add to your argument that the security cameras in the immediate neighborhood did not show any activity of a stranger present during the estimated time of the murder. While that is sort of negative evidence, it would lend itself to looking at Boyd Richards and not some unknown intruder. Besides, I haven't yet finished my investigation of Boyd and his 'babe on the side' potential. Maybe we'll have additional motive."

Looking back at the chief, Sheila said, "There, you see? This detective is looking in the right direction. Let's draw up a complaint. I'll take this to the grand jury and get him indicted."

As Worten left Sheila's office, he chewed on her last words. *What a laugh! The running joke in law enforcement is the grand jury would indict a ham sandwich if instructed by the prosecutor. There's gonna be trouble ahead.* An afterthought: *Gilhooley, you little suck-up!*

CHAPTER
Thirteen

The world stands aside to let anyone pass
who knows where he is going.

Goethe – German writer and statesman

One week later in a Union County Courtroom, mid-morning

Mack **glanced at his vibrating iPhone again**, palming it low between his knees so the jury couldn't sense his indifference to the witness on the stand. Glaring at the phone, he thought, *I already answered it once, ya dope!* It was the second text in five minutes from Avery Reddy, criminal defense lawyer — and general pain in the ass when people didn't jump through hoops for him. *Big case, big case,* Mack silently mocked the text. *They're all big to somebody!*

Mack just "celebrated" the anniversary of his eighteenth year in his private investigation business by pulling an all-night surveillance with retired state trooper and associate Bob Higgins. Then he had to make a quick change and get to an early court appearance to offer testimony in a fraud case. He was approaching burnout.

An hour later, descending the courthouse steps and loosening his tie, he spoke into his phone, "Okay, ya got me now. Jeez, Avery, I was in Frankel's court and couldn't step out. Ya know how he is about any stirring in court when somebody's on the stand. What's this big case that couldn't wait?"

Attorney Reddy, always given to the dramatic, said, "We're on the edge now, buddy. I picked up the Richards murder case, and I need you to get right on it." Mack had already read about the case in the *Courier News* and agreed with Avery, *This IS a big one!*

"Okay, I'll be there in a couple hours or so. Gotta stop in at the office first."

Mack made a quick stop back at his Central Jersey office on Route 22 in Greenbrook. He read over the report his assistant Inez had just finished typing and signed it.

"Avery Reddy called—as usual, beside himself. Something about a big case," Inez said, handing Mack a yellow Post-it note. She added, "You need sleep; you look like crap!"

"Nezzie, we already talked. I'm off to his office now. Give Higgins a call, but not till later on this afternoon. He didn't get any sleep, either. Tell him we are on the Richards case—he'll know what that means—and ask him to come in early tomorrow so we can kick it around." With a teasing wink, he left his middle-aged assistant with her bright lipstick and over-tweezed eyebrows frowning, as she reached for her ringing desk phone. Her eyes rolling, she sing-songed, "Mackey Investigations, always here to serve you."

Navigating the dark green Range Rover around the many idiots eternally on their mobile phones, Mack mused aloud, "The *Courier* quoted the prosecutor's office as having confidence in their evidence against Boyd Richards. We're in for a ride, for sure, Avery... for sure." He pulled into the lawyer's parking lot in Westfield in under a half hour.

Avery Reddy came to his feet when Mack was ushered into the lawyer's plush conference room. Mack had been here before and was not at all awestruck with the row upon row of legal books on the shelves that lined two walls of the room. He wondered which of the many cases he'd worked on for this lawyer paid for the expensive oriental rugs or the gaudy leather chairs surrounding the solid mahogany glass-topped table.

Mack, forever nurturing his casual contempt for lawyerly self-importance—and just to add to his customary sarcasm—said, "Avery, I've always wanted to ask you if you get to use all those books, or are they just there to impress?

"Let's cut your usual bullshit and get down to business. Take a seat and start reviewing my file. There's not much here yet, because the prosecutor's discovery package won't be here until Monday. But we need to get started, anyway." Avery Reddy, a chubby, red-faced, fifty-eight-year-old, was actually a very good lawyer in spite of his penchant for annoying just about everyone with his nervous and impatient mannerisms. He and Mack had formed this delicate back-and-forth bantering relationship over the years, but each had deep respect for the other's particular skills: Avery's quick grasp of the facts and an ability to have them speak for his client; and Mack's uncanny read on people and investigative thoroughness—even if the latter did drive Avery wild sometimes.

"Okay, here goes." Mack flipped open the file with a deep sigh and began reviewing its contents.

CHAPTER
Fourteen

A friend is one before whom I may think aloud.

Ralph Waldo Emerson – American poet

Mack's office, the next day, 9:25 a.m.

"**Hey, Bob, thanks for coming.**" Mack partially stood up from his desk as the two friends shook hands. Bob Higgins flopped into the opposing chair, and sighing loudly, said, "Well, this is another fine mess you've gotten us into, Stanley!"

Sergeant Bob Higgins had been through just about every possible scenario during his twenty years with the New Jersey State Police. From shootouts and fatal car crashes to high-speed chases and scraping body parts off railroad tracks, he was no stranger to death and dismemberment. At fifty-five, he kept in shape by working out regularly and keeping to his Brenda-imposed healthy diet. At just under six feet with a ruddy complexion and thin moustache, Higgins spent his off-time fishing in Round Valley Reservoir out in Hunterdon County. Forever the wise-cracker, Bob would quip, "At first, it took some doin' to throw a fish back into the water. I'm used to keeping what I catch... and throwing 'em into the back of a trooper car."

"Yeah, Bob, this one is getting a lot of press, and Avery's beside himself. He says his reputation is on the line. He's definitely under a full head of steam."

"So, what's the skinny, Mack?"

"I read over Avery's preliminary, and here's the way it goes: the prosecutor recused himself because he and Boyd Richards are country club buds. The assistant prosecutor took over and is out for blood—our client's blood, of course; but it's mostly because she wants Raymond's job or something bigger. Boyd was arrested Saturday at the hotel where he and the kids are staying over near the interstate. Someone tipped off the press—guess who? So, the perp walk got on the evening news. Not exactly what Boyd Richards was looking for." Higgins was shaking his head.

Mack continued, "He was bonded out, because, as Avery so smoothly put it to the judge, 'Your Honor, my client is an attorney, deeply involved in the community. He has never been arrested, is not a flight risk and is anxious to put this nonsensical charge behind him so he and his children can grieve for the loss of their beloved wife and mother. Judge, it's all smoke and mirrors and the circumstantial evidence leads nowhere. I smell political opportunity here, and I am looking right at her!'"

Laughing, Mack continued, "Higgins, I'm tellin' ya, I've never seen anything like it in a courtroom before. Sheila Cummings jumped to her feet and literally screamed at Avery. She actually called him an asshole right out in the courtroom! The judge rapped his gavel so hard it broke, and the court reporter almost fell off his chair. The media loved it."

"You mean Sheila, Queen of the Jungle, herself? Oh, I guess that was Sheena... never mind. But I didn't know she made it to first chair. You're right, pal, this is gonna be a circus. But give with the facts. Just what have they got on our hero?"

"As Avery said, it's pretty much all circumstantial, but you know as well as I do, that's all it takes to convict if the prosecutor plays it right and can cast the defendant in a bad light with innuendo."

"Ah, yes, the old innuendo. Stickin' it right up there in-your-endo!"

"That's about it, my friend. We've got our work cut out for us. Here's what they have: first, the cops found out that the victim, Callie Richards, was having an affair with a young tennis stud. One of the neighbors—I think her name is Hargey or something like it—finally admitted to one of the detectives that she set her friend up with the kid 'cause they both thought Boyd was doin' one of his office lovelies. The operating theory is that Boyd found out about it, and during an argument he knifed his wife to death. In the absence of any forensics pointing elsewhere, and with no other motive in sight, they concentrated on our boy."

Higgins, nodding his understanding, asked, "So, what's our game plan?"

"Avery wants us to meet with his client this afternoon before anything else. Remember, Boyd Richards is a lawyer himself. He mostly does corporate deals, not criminal defense; nevertheless, you know what this will be like with him second-guessing everything."

"Yeah, typical lawyer. What are we doing after that?"

"Several things: First, we gotta go to the scene and get up to speed. Next, Avery says more discovery will be in on Monday, so we need to go over that.

"Yeah, sounds good. But what about going back to the neighborhood and banging on doors. You know how lazy the cops can be once they come up with something. They never go back and finish up."

"Good, you start on that tomorrow. It would be great if you can come up with something new."

"If... if wishes were horses, beggars would ride. If horse turds were biscuits, they'd eat till they died. Sorry, guess I'm overusing that one."

Mack smiled and teased, "Ass-hole! See ya later this afternoon at Avery's."

CHAPTER
Fifteen

A leader is a dealer in hope.

Napoleon Bonaparte – French military and political leader

Lawyer Reddy's office, 3:00 p.m., the same day.

*A*ttorney **Avery Reddy sat at the head** of the long glass-topped conference table, his file sliding back and forth between his nervous index fingers. Mack and Higgins sat to his right and Boyd Richards to his left.

Avery kicked it off. "What we have here is strictly a political hit job based solely on circumstantial evidence. All we have to do is follow that line and we can't lose."

"Avery, stating the obvious was always your strong suit, but, if you think I am going to take this lying down by letting that bitch smear me with innuendo, you're nuts!" Boyd Richards was just getting warmed up.

Mack caught Higgins mouthing, "Innuendo" and shook his head, suppressing a smile.

"Well, let's see what the investigators say," said Avery, turning to Mack and Higgins with lifted eyebrows.

Mack cleared his throat and stood up. He slowly walked around the table and said, "Let's recap: The prosecution has a statement from Grace Harjes to the effect that Mrs. Richards was having an affair."

Boyd Richards exploded, "That's bullshit, and I won't hear that spoken here again. My Callie would never..."

"Nevertheless, Mr. Richards, that's where they are going for motive, and it's a strong one," said Mack, looking back to Avery for support.

"Correct," declared Avery, and before Richardson could continue his protest, he raised his hand to stop him. "Continue, Mack."

"Next, extensive witness interviews on the block, including a man who spent the entire day in front of his home, could not produce anyone who saw any cars at your residence. That is further backed up with security tapes from cameras from the three houses with the best views. Then we have your inability to independently confirm your whereabouts the day of the murder."

Mack then turned to Avery. "Look, you may think this is *only* a circumstantial case, but the facts make it much more than circumstantial." Higgins nodded in agreement.

Mack's intensity caught Avery and Richards by surprise. Avery asked, "What are you getting at?"

"Mr. Richards, there are powers in play here—people who are really out to get you. That means fair play and 'innocent until proven guilty' goes out the window. Do you understand you are a target defendant? You are the jewel in the crown of an up-and-coming assistant prosecutor. You are the target of another politician who doesn't want you to run against him again. Get it?"

Richards started to say something, but Mack shut him up. "And I am not done yet." Turning back to Avery, he said, "You better get used to the idea this case will be tried in the press, and you'd better get your best camera shots in when you can."

Avery, trying to recover control of the meeting, said, "Listen, all of you, I have been trying cases like this for thirty years. Our legal system is set up to prevent convictions without proper evidence. There are rules." He ended with a haughty, "We need to play by those rules!"

Mack turned to Higgins. "Bob, we discussed this earlier."

"Yeah," Bob was staring out the side window. "I fear the only way out of this is to catch the son-of-a-bitch ourselves."

Avery's eyes rolled back in his head, "Don't any of you understand? They have to prove their case, we don't have to catch anybody! It's not our job; the cops do that. Why can't I get through to you?"

Boyd Richards had been watching the back-and-forth and listening intently. "Maybe he's right, Avery. What if the cops go along with the politics? Jesus! I'm screwed!"

CHAPTER
Sixteen

It is the theory that decides what can be observed.

Albert Einstein – German-born theoretical physicist

Friday, 9:45 a.m.

When investigator Bob Higgins went to the Manor Hill Road neighborhood, he found most neighbors uncomfortable with any further interviews. They had been worked over fairly well by the police investigators and said so. In variation, most responded to Higgins like this: "Look, I told all I know to the police. Check with them. I don't have the time for this, and if you are working for Boyd Richards, you can get off my porch right now. I don't help killers!"

When Higgins arrived at the Harjes home, however, it was different. Dan Harjes answered the door. Up to this point, reported interviews had been with Grace—not Dan. "So, Mr. Harjes, can I come in and have a sit-down with you for a few minutes?"

"I guess so," he said tentatively and with a furrowed brow. "Let's go out onto the patio."

Once settled, Higgins asked Dan, "What was your relationship with Boyd?"

"We were golf buddies, that's all," said an uncomfortable and fidgeting Dan Harjes.

"Well, I guess you talked about things—family, work, kids— you know?" Dan's body language led Higgins to believe he was on the verge of a breakthrough.

"Not really. Not much, anyway," Dan said while staring hard at the bricks between his alternately tapping feet.

Seeing that proverbial opening, Higgins leaned forward, "C'mon, Dan. You can tell me. I'm not the police. I'm working for Boyd and his kids. What happened to this family is a tragedy and you know it. I can see you know something. C'mon, man."

Dan nodded his head and relented. "Gracie and I went through some hard times a couple of years ago. I strayed—if you know what I mean—and Gracie got back at me by doing the same. We realized how stupid we had been. I mean, the kids and all. So, we went into counseling and it worked great for us. We are closer than ever now.

Higgins nodded. "Go on."

"Well, I made a wisecrack to Gracie that I saw Boyd with a young woman. Actually, I referred to her as 'a young cutie.' They were having a drink in an uptown restaurant. I swear, I didn't think she would go and tell Callie."

"Do you know who this young woman is?"

"No, it was just in passing, and I'm pretty sure they didn't see me. I didn't want to embarrass him, ya know? But...uh, there's more."

"Go on, you're doing great," counseled Higgins.

"Well, here's the tough part: Gracie said she introduced Callie to the same guy she..." Dan couldn't finish the sentence. He added, "She blames herself for setting Callie up with him. She thinks Boyd found out and... well, you know the rest."

"I see. Would that be the young tennis pro?"

"Yeah. All I know is his first name. They call him 'Johnny Boy,' and he's the tennis pro at the club."

"Dan, was there anything in their relationship that could lead you to believe Boyd would ever hurt Callie?"

"Never. That's why I was so shocked the police arrested him. I guess he must've found out about Callie and that tennis kid somehow."

Higgins cut in, "But you don't know that, right? I mean you never discussed anything like that with Boyd, did ya?"

"No, no. Not at all."

Back in his car, Higgins made notes of his interview. He thought it better not to do so in front of Dan. The guy was nervous enough. *Let's see: Dan believed Boyd was having an affair of his own with, in Dan's words: 'a young cutie in his office.' Maybe it was just an impression from seeing Boyd in a restaurant with the cutie, but his implication was clear. Gotta check it out. He knew that Callie was having a good old time with Johnny Boy. Enough motive for either Boyd or Johnny Boy.*

Later that day, both Higgins and Mack went back to Manor Hill Road and took a walk around the outside of the Richards home. The blood stain was still visible on the concrete near the pool. The lounge chair had been folded and was leaning against the pool house nearby. Otherwise, it looked like any well-cared-for backyard in an upscale neighborhood.

The two walked around slowly, taking everything in. "You know, Bob, the cops must have checked the security cameras all over this neighborhood; yet I haven't heard of any departures or arrivals that would put the killer here at the house at that time."

"True, but, after all, this is the Richards house. Boyd could've been here and not left for work yet."

"No, I don't think so. This happened early afternoon, during working hours. This guy is a workaholic. Can you see him hanging around here all morning, then stabbing his wife from behind?" Mack's attention was drawn to the back of the yard. "Wait just a minute... back in the car."

Higgins drove around the block behind the Richards home. Mack blurted, "Stop. Back up. See what I see?"

Yeah…YEAH, that's it!

Higgins backed up and drove his van into the driveway of a house with a Realtor's for-sale sign on the front lawn. Not only that, the house appeared vacant, as there were no curtains visible on the windows. "This is how a perp could get to her without even entering her street. He would've seen just what we are seeing. Who would question someone walking around or a strange car in the driveway of a house for sale? Let's get out and take a look around."

In another minute the two found themselves behind the vacant house and in a thickly foliated area along the rear property line, which backs up to the Richards' property. "Jeez, Bob, he could've crouched down here and waited for her to come out in the yard. The weather was nice, and the Richards have a pool. Don't people with pools spend time in their backyards?" They looked around on the ground, but there was nothing indicating someone had been there: no footprints, no broken vegetation, no gum wrappers… no luck.

"I'm beginning to think our Boyd might not be a murderer. I don't like him, but…"

"I know," Mack cut in. "Next stop: Johnny Boy. Now there's a possibility."

CHAPTER
Seventeen

Honesty is as rare as a man without self-pity.
Stephen Vincent Benét – American poet and writer

Same day, 4:10 p.m.

*M*ack called his assistant, Inez, and instructed her to call the tennis club and see if tennis pro Johnny Boy was at work. She called back. "Mack, he's off today. Called in sick. I did get his last name, though: Campbell. Got his address, too." Delighted, as always with his assistant's work, Mack said, "You are a peach, Nezzie."

Higgins and Mack pulled up to small loft-type house off a lane in New Providence. Johnny Boy's apartment was in a building that years prior was a horse barn with an apartment above for the caretaker. The barn area, now a garage, still had two horse stalls, but there was room for the small red sports car backed in. There was a front door with a staircase leading to the second-floor apartment next to the garage. The bell didn't work, so Mack pounded on the door.

"Hey, knock it off! Who are you and wadda ya want?" the young tennis pro barked, with only half of his face showing through the partially opened door.

"We're here to talk to you about Callie Richards, Johnny. We know about her relationship with you. We're not the police. How 'bout coming out so we can talk."

"I don't know what you're talkin' about. Go away."

"No problem," replied Mack, "I'll just call my buddy in the prosecutor's office. I'm sure you'd rather talk to him."

"Wait." Johnny Campbell opened the door and stepped out wearing tennis shorts and flip-flops. He was tall, with dark hair and, as one would expect of an athlete, in good physical shape. "Yes, Callie and I had a thing," he said, shaking his head in disbelief. "She broke up with me the day before she was murdered. I still can't believe it. Who would hurt that lovely soul?"

"Well," said Mack, "you would be a person of interest, wouldn't you?"

Frowning, Johnny said, "Yeah, I suppose you could think that. I went over all that with that detective the other day," Johnny said impatiently. "Gilhooley was his name, I think. Listen, there's no way I would've killed her. We weren't in love or anything like that. It was just sex. Hey, guys, my job has me surrounded by rich, good-lookin' old babes. You really think I need a complicated relationship?"

Mack and Higgins exchanged sour looks, then Mack forged on. "We're private investigators working for Mr. Richards, Callie's husband. We are just trying to find out all we can, and I think you and Callie would've done some talking about things, like her marriage and such. So, why don't you help us out here?"

"Like I told the detective, Callie and I met at the club and had our get-togethers here," he explained, gesturing up to his loft. "We met about six or seven times in the past two months."

Mack and Higgins continued their interview of Campbell for the next half hour. In the end, Campbell was cooperative. He showed them where Callie would park amidst the cars in the insurance company's lot and walk up the alley to his apartment.

As they left, Higgins asked, "So, Mack, what's your take on this guy?"

"Nah, you really think he would even be around a couple of days after brutally killing Callie? He tries to be cool, but you can see right through it. He doesn't have the stones to commit murder." As an afterthought, however, he said, "But Avery will eat him alive if he gets his paws on him. He will say, 'Mack, thanks for handing me someone else with motive. Good job!'"

Higgins frowned, "Yeah. Avery."

CHAPTER
Eighteen

A hateful act is the transference to another of the degradation we bear in ourselves.
Simone Weil – French philosopher and political activist

Same day, 4:30 p.m.

Bruce was getting used to the comings and goings of the insurance company employees. He was still a little uptight about that detective's interest in the alley and, with not much else to do, continued his stakeout. "…seventy-eight, seventy-nine, eighty." Finishing another set of pushups, he crawled back up onto his roost in the back of the van. The exercise helped him pass the time. It kept him focused and, of course, it kept the demons at bay.

"Who the hell is this now?" Bruce stiffened. Through his binoculars, he could make out two older men and a younger one wearing tennis shorts coming down the alley in Bruce's general direction, though still more than two hundred feet away. The younger one was apparently explaining something, which included pointing back from where they had come, then out into the parking lot where Bruce was parked.

"More cops. I don't like this at all," he said under his breath. "Who is this kid and what did he see? Maybe he saw me bump into the blonde." He bit his lip and shook his head. "Can't have that!"

The two older detectives walked away together, as the younger man walked back up the alley and made a quick right turn. Bruce waited until the detectives drove off, then slowly drove up the alley, himself. Near the end, he caught a movement off to his right in a driveway. The kid was wiping down the front end of a red MGB convertible sticking out of a garage. Bruce came up with a plan.

"Now, that's one beautiful car. Yours?"

Johnny Campbell was surprised by the voice behind him. "Yes, it is. Who are you?"

"Leonard Howe. Just moved in around the corner." He offered a friendly hand to Johnny. "What year is this? I have a '68, but not nearly in the same shape as this one," Bruce continued, feigning admiration for the car.

"Yeah, she's my baby. A '66. I picked it up last year from, uh, a friend whose husband hated it. Let's put it this way... a lady friend," said Johnny, with a touch of a smugness and a wink.

"Mind if I take a closer look?" Bruce moved into the garage toward the rear of the vehicle, all the while swooning over the car. The further he went into the garage the darker it got. He also looked around carefully for what he would need.

"Well, I suppose," said Johnny. "You can look, but it's not for sale." He bragged, "I get a lot of lookers."

"I bet you do," Bruce said, nodding in mock approval. Suddenly, and with feigned concern, he continued according to plan, "Whoa, did you know you have a nasty scratch back here on the boot?"

Johnny took the bait and rushed over. "Where?" he said, leaning over at the back of the car. "I don't see any…"

The struggle was brief. "You won't be talking to anybody else, pal," said Bruce as he tied off the rope to the bumper of the sports car. He glanced up at Johnny, still swaying back and forth, his eyes bugged-out and a stream of urine running down his left leg. *Funny*, he thought, *if you have to snuff somebody, might as well do it up close and get a thrill out of it. I just can't see using a gun. Too loud and no… personal bonding*. That last thought gave him a giggle. Giving the rope's end a final yank, Bruce walked away. He looked up and down the alley before entering and coldly sniggered, "I hate loose ends!"

CHAPTER
Nineteen

From error to error one discovers the entire truth.

Sigmund Freud – Austrian founder of psychoanalysis

Next day, early afternoon

*M*ack rode up the tower elevator in the Union County Prosecutor's Detective Bureau on the ninth floor of the Union County Complex in Elizabeth. The ride was reminiscent of the many times he took that elevator years ago as a young county investigator.

"Chief, there's a private investigator to see you. A Mr. Mackey. Should I send him in?"

Chief Worten rose from his chair. "Mack, how good to see you. What a surprise!" he said enthusiastically. Then, in a more solemn tone, "Sorry to hear about Margie. That must have been tough."

Mack ignored the last comment. "Good to see you too, old buddy. The place has changed a little." He looked around at all the computer stations and the modern office atmosphere. "Looks like quite the operation compared to when we were grunts here, no?"

"Hey, gotta keep up with the times and the crimes." Worten, realizing he had cracked a kind of joke, gave a chuckle. "Sit." He gestured to a chair across from his desk. "Is this a good-old-days visit or something business-like?"

"Business."

"Richards?"

Mack nodded his head, but Worten frowned. "Mack, you know I can't discuss this with you..."

Mack cut him off, waving his hand and saying, "I know, I know, but you can listen, right?"

"Does Avery know you're here?"

"No, but this is a special circumstance, my friend. I hope you will at least give me a few minutes—off the record, if you want. Avery doesn't allow himself to think in any other terms than a defense counsel. You know what I mean."

"Yeah. I deal with the opposite mentality with the lawyers on this side. So, shoot."

Mack explained what he and Higgins had discovered the day before. "I think you need to take a second look at this, Bill. Anyone could've gotten into that backyard without being seen at the front. In fact, the lounge chair was positioned perfectly for the perp. The argument that the neighborhood cameras didn't show anyone no longer holds water. Another thing: this tennis pro looks like a person of interest in my book. She broke up with him the day before. Bob and I didn't go too deep with him. Didn't want to step on your case, but you really ought to check further into this."

"Wait a minute, Mack. Just because someone could come up behind her from the direction of the neighboring backyard doesn't rule out hubby, and you know it."

"No, but it makes it nonexclusive, doesn't it? Any defense attorney would see it as adding reasonable doubt. C'mon, man. Think about it."

Worten's secretary stuck her head in, "Important call, Mr. Worten."

"Not now. Take a message."

"You better take this one. Another dead body."

Chief Worten signaled a pause with one upright finger toward Mack and picked up his phone. "Worten here." He listened for a moment. As his face darkened, he peered up at Mack over his reading glasses, a shocked look apparent. He cradled the phone, and after a deep sigh, he said, "You ain't gonna believe this, Mack. Your tennis boy just hung himself!"

Chief Worten and Mack parked in the alley and walked past the two patrol cars and Gilhooley's unmarked Plymouth. When they made the turn into the short driveway, they saw the medical examiner's van parked farther ahead. Dr. Restin, his head cocked to the side, was looking up at Johnny Boy, his neck now stretched by the rope. A forensic technician was taking photographs. Gilhooley looked up from his note-taking. "Hi, boss. I came over here to interview this guy again. As I told you, I found out from that Harjes woman that he was Callie Richards's boyfriend—and this is what I found."

Worten, now senior man on scene, took over. "Okay, Gilhooley, what do we have here? Looks like suicide, so far, no?"

"Looks like it, Chief." Gilhooley walked around inside the barn-turned-garage, gesturing as he went. "He took an old rope from one of the horse stalls, looped it, threw it up and over the beam, tied it to the bumper, then stepped up on this stool and jumped off. We haven't found a note yet. He might have felt bad about his girlfriend's murder or, for that matter, he could be her killer and it got to him, so... either way."

"Okay, let's cut him down." Turning to the young detective, Worten said, "You'd better take a look in his apartment, too. Never know what we might find, like a note or a knife?"

Mack chimed in, "Wait a minute, Bill. Can Doc and I take a closer look? I know I'm not here officially, but Doc is."

Worten shrugged and began looking around deeper into the garage.

Mack and Doc Restin moved in closer to the still-suspended Johnny Boy. Doc started the conversation, "Probably dead more than sixteen, less than thirty hours, judging by rigor and lividity." He pointed to the deep purple color of the victim's legs. "Gravity has blood pooling in the lower extremities."

While Doc Restin continued with the pathology lesson, Mack took note of the other evidence. The rope was of the same kind as the rest of the pile nearby. It was old-fashioned hemp, left there, no doubt, by whomever was the last person to keep horses in the barn. He took a closer look at the rope suspending Johnny Boy. It was tied to the bumper of the sports car in two half-hitches. It then went up to and over a barn beam near the ceiling, then down to the noose around Johnny Boy's neck. Mack picked up the stool and put it underneath the body. He drew back.

"Doc, take a look at this." Mack was incredulous.

"Yikes!" said Doc. "How the hell can you fall or jump off a stool if it's too short to reach your feet after you're hanging there...and with your neck stretched?"

"And how 'bout this?" said Mack excitedly. He was pointing to the rope between the bumper and the overhead beam. The old-fashioned rope had what could only be described as "hairs" protruding out in all directions, unlike modern smooth ropes. The hairs on one side of the rope between the bumper and the beam all pointed back toward the beam. But from the beam down to the victim's neck, the hairs stuck out uniformly on all sides. Mack pointed with his index finger, tracing the path of the disturbed hairs and then down to the noose area. Doc got it and nodded his head.

Doc hollered, "Hey Bill. You better get over here!"

The three of them set up an experiment. They took one of the old ropes and looped it over the beam. "Doc, you hold tight to this end while Bill and I lift you up." The hairs on the rope between the beam and where Bill and Mack pulled were bent back in the same manner as the rope from the bumper to the beam where Johnny still hung, but not bent between the beam and where Doc was holding on. A closer look at the rope at the bumper in the area of the knot showed identical drag markings starting the right distance from the knot, all of which pointed to someone hauling Johnny Boy up toward the beam.

Chief Worten, now energized, barked, "Dammit! This is a staged suicide scene. We've got a murder case here! Bring that technician back in with his camera, a ruler and plastic evidence bags. Gilhooley, make a drawing of this to go with the photographs."

Mack overheard Gilhooley say, "No problem. How 'bout that, Chief? Two murders in the same week just a hundred feet apart."

"What are you talking about?" both Worten and Mack asked, almost in unison.

"Yeah, that guy that fell down the stairs in the insurance company. You remember, Chief? Doc, here, changed it to a murder? That insurance company is just down the alley."

Chief Worten, eyes widening, moaned, "You mean to tell me you've waited till now to spring this on me?"

"Yeah, well the addresses are on two different streets that back up to each other. I didn't get it until I remembered walking around in the alley, but from the other direction. Sorry, Chief."

Worten and Mack walked back up the alley toward the front door of the insurance company. Worten said, "Let's go in and check this out some more."

Stopping short with his hand on Worten's elbow, Mack said, "Wait a minute, Bill. I told you Bob Higgins and I interviewed Johnny back there yesterday—and he's found swinging today? Don't you think that's a little coincidental? Also, you say there's another homicide—days earlier—just down this alley in the insurance company? What's that all about? Another coincidence?"

"Hmm. I don't believe in coincidences either. What's on your mind?"

"I think we need to put together a timeline and have a sit-down before we go off half-cocked." Mack looked around the area uncomfortably. "Also, I would not like to think the perp was watching me and Higgins yesterday, and that's what brought about the kid's demise."

Walking back down the alley to Johnny's driveway, Worten observed, "There's just one thing we're forgetting, Mack. This isn't the old days, and we ain't partners anymore. We're on opposite sides of the Richards case. We can't work on this together, and you know it."

"Okay, I get that," said Mack, "but I can go ahead on this myself. Here's an idea: I will work on the timeline and feed it to you. Let's keep this a suicide as far as the public is concerned. No need to let our perp think we're onto him, right? That's just in case these cases are really connected."

"Sounds good. Now I have to get Gilhooley and Doc onboard before we take another step. Have fun explaining this to Avery," said Worten, sarcastically. "He's gonna hate losing Johnny Boy as an alternative defendant to Boyd Richards."

"Yeah, Avery…"

CHAPTER
Twenty

Imagination is the eye of the soul.

Joseph Joubert – French essayist and moralist

Tuesday, 3:50 p.m.

*A*ttorney Avery Reddy stood on the steps of the Union County Courthouse in Elizabeth and spoke directly into the camera. "The prosecutor on this case is being uncooperative and I will be forced to go to the judge unless she fulfills her discovery requirements. The defense is entitled to all—and I mean all—police reports. My file is very thin after more than a month of waiting."

The reporter asked, "Mr. Reddy, we know you have been making claims of political retribution, as well as the lack of forensic evidence. Just what is it you believe they are holding back?"

"I can tell you this, Marsha, if they had any real evidence, like forensics, it would be out here and they would be gloating over it. Either they are holding back, which is wrong, *or* they don't have anything—and that last one would be my bet. Sorry, I have to move on."

Turning back to the camera, the reporter closed her segment, "This is Marsha Gruener reporting from the steps of the Union County Courthouse in Elizabeth, New Jersey. This Boyd Richards case will surely be one to watch as it plays out over time. Back to you in the studio, Tom."

Same day, 6:10 p.m.

Bruce was glued to the television in his trailer. "So, it's forensic evidence you need, huh?" He went outside and—first checking back and forth for prying eyes—reached under the back of the trailer to his secret spot and pulled out a rag-wrapped object. Back in the trailer, he held the knife up to the sunlight streaming through the trailer's skylight. "Oh yeah! There's still a lot of blood on here." He cuddled down into his recliner and closed his eyes. He hefted the weight of the knife and assessed its balance. It felt like an old friend. 'That's not a knife. *This* is a knife!' he laughed, mimicking Crocodile Dundee. He allowed himself a whimsical trip back to poolside and felt a rush plunging the knife into the center of that woman's chest again. *We are looking at each other upside down now—our faces inches apart. I stab! You're struggling up off the chair and falling onto your back near the pool. You're wide-eyed and in shock. Remember me, Blondie? You do. I see recognition in your eyes. You're fading. I should make this look like something personal. Here's some more, baby... again, again, and again. There you go. A tear is trickling down your cheek. It pools in your ear.*

The euphoric fantasy fading, he turned back to formulating his plan aloud. "I'm so glad I paid attention during those rookie police classes." But an uneasy thought crept into his consciousness: *What is happening to me? I've killed three people in the last few days, and I don't feel anything for them. I've changed. It's all about survival now. Survival!*

Intending to give the prosecution what it needed, and to *"screw that political hack husband,"* he changed clothes and drove up to Summit toward the Manor Hill neighborhood. He stopped at the 7-Eleven convenience store on Central Avenue and went into action.

"Good afternoon. I am with the security system you guys have up here. I just need to take down some of the serial numbers on the recorder. We're updating our inventory. I'll only take a minute." The clerk was so busy with a line of coffee and donut customers, she simply waved him into the back room. Bruce stifled a grin and thought, *What a good idea to wear the suit today. Why do people fall over so easily for a suit and a smile?*

When the coffee and lottery line cleared, he asked the clerk, "Are you guys still on a two-week loop here? I didn't bother to check."

"No, no. The boss is only interested in shoplifters. It loops automatically once a week."

Bruce left satisfied and waited eight days, assured that his visit was no longer on tape. He then went back into the 7-Eleven and directly into the men's room. He locked the door and took a deep breath. Kneeling down on the floor, he took out the blood-stained knife and, where the floor met the wall under the sink, he gently scraped some of Callie Richards' dried blood chips onto the light blue tile. With a small brush, he made sure most of it remained in the cracked area of the grout, so no cleaning up would ruin his plan. The forensic handbook from the police academy had been helpful, especially the Chapter on "The Collection and Preservation of Blood Samples for Analysis."

Now, here's where my plan gets a little hairy, he reasoned. He waited eight more days, then launched.

The sergeant behind the high desk at the Summit Police Department wheeled his chair around and asked officiously, "How can I help you?"

"I, uh... think I have some information on that lady that was killed a couple of months ago," he offered, looking around nervously — part of the act. "Am I in the right place?"

The sergeant dropped the attitude and asked, "What kind of information?"

"I saw the guy they arrested on television the other day. He's the same guy I saw in a 7-Eleven store a while back. He had blood on his hands, so..."

"You stay right there, buddy!" The sergeant made a hurried call and within seconds a detective joined Bruce in front of the tall desk. The detective and the sergeant shared a skeptical glance, as Bruce was guided to a small conference room nearby,

"First," said the detective, pulling out a notebook and pen, "please give me your name and address." This was all too routine for the detective. *His questioning will be mechanical. But only for a little while longer,* thought Gordon, up until now, referred to as "Bruce."

"My name is Gordon Krone, and I live in trailer number 16 at the Sunshine Trailer Court in Union. It's just off Springfield Avenue."

"Date of birth, Gordon?"

"October 24th in 1981. My birthday is coming up in a couple of weeks."

"Okay, you told the sergeant you know something about a murder? Oh, and I hope you don't mind if I record our conversation."

"No problem. Uh, yes. I stopped for a Coke at the 7-Eleven on Central Avenue and used the men's room while I was there. I'm unemployed and I was out looking for a job at the time. By the way, I am looking for a law enforcement job again. I am certified through the Union County Police Academy. I was a C.O. at Rahway for a while." Gordon paused, so that could sink in.

"Uh huh. Go on." The detective squirmed in his chair. Gordon could sense his impatience.

"Anyway, as I came out of the men's room, a man bumped into me. He was pushing his way in. I was as close to him as I am to you and I can tell you, he was upset." Gordon went on, raising his voice an octave, thus heightening the drama. "I couldn't help seeing he held his hands up like this..." Gordon demonstrated with his hands up near his chest in a grotesque position, "... and I saw there was blood all over his hands and a little bit here on the side of his face. I thought it strange at the time, but didn't have anything to connect it to. I thought maybe he cut himself outside or something. Then I saw that guy on the news the other day." Gordon shook his head in feigned disbelief. "Man-oh-man, I knew I had to come down here."

"I see, Gordon, but are you sure it was blood you saw?"

"Well, it sure looked like it. It was red and wet and smeary. It didn't look like paint."

"Are you sure it was the same guy you saw on television? You know, people look different on the screen than in real life. There was some time in between, so..."

"Oh, it was him, all right. For sure. That head of hair? Oh, yeah."

"Gordon, may I see your New Jersey driver's license?"

Gordon expected this. He had decided to use his real name because, as a witness for the prosecution, he would surely be vetted carefully. He was also confident that his former status as a corrections officer and an academy graduate would lend legitimacy to his persona. He dug his license out and obediently handed it over. "Sure, here it is." Gordon was having fun toying with the detective. *This is only gonna get better. I'm gonna have fun with all these guys that are too good to hire me. And convicting that politician... well, that'll be icing on the cake!*

"Wait here, Gordon."

After ten minutes, the detective hustled back in and said, "Well, Gordon, you just might be an important witness in a big case." All portent of tedium had left the detective. His new attitude was buoyant.

"Really?" Gordon said, affecting naivety.

"Yeah, you and I are going to take a ride down to Elizabeth to the county prosecutor's office. You need to tell them what you told me."

"Oh, you don't handle it locally?"

"No, I mostly deal with burglaries, assaults, druggies, and the like. It's the prosecutor's office that takes on the big cases like this." The detective was solicitous and Gordon saw his story had taken hold. *This is really gonna be fun!*

"I see. Can I leave my car in your parking lot?"

"Sure, Gordon. Sure" On the way out, the detective and the desk sergeant again exchanged knowing looks; their eye-to-eye more appreciative this time.

CHAPTER
Twenty-One

Truth never dies, but lives a wretched life.
Yiddish proverb

iggins called in to Avery immediately following his interview with Dan Harjes. He emphasized that Dan had told the police about "the young cutie" and that it was important to determine who she was and the nature of the relationship. Avery went over it with Boyd Richards and got back to Higgins. "Bob, Boyd tells me it was a routine interview he had with a recent law school graduate looking for a position in the firm."

"Don't you think it a bit odd to do that over drinks in a bar setting?" asked Bob.

"I asked him about that. He said he likes to see how someone is going to handle themselves in a social setting rather than in the office atmosphere. His corporate clients often meet under those conditions, so..."

"Okay. So, should I leave that alone now?"

"No. Her name is Gail Miller. She was hired, but only stayed a few months. She left to work in a law firm in Florida, he thinks. Check it out and if you can find her, go there and get a statement. You know what to do: clear up their relationship, why she left, etcetera."

Higgins called Mack at his office, "Avery wants me to find the girl Boyd was seen with having drinks. He thinks she is a lawyer in Florida now. Would you ask Nezzie to check the Florida Bar Association for a Gail Miller... late twenties? Then I'm supposed to go there and get a statement."

Bob Higgins walked down the jetway at Southwest Florida International Airport in Fort Myers and met with Gail Miller in a nearby Starbucks in the terminal. "Thanks for seeing me, Ms. Miller." His first thought was, *Dan Harjes is right, she is a cutie.* Gail was direct in her answers and made it clear to Higgins that the meeting she had with Boyd Richards was strictly business.

She added, "You know, of course, that a Detective Gilhooley has already been here, right?"

"No. We didn't know. How did that go?" Higgins answered, a bit surprised.

"I told him the same thing about my interview meeting with Mr. Richards. But he wanted to know everything about what went on in the Richards Law Firm. You know, relationships between employees."

Higgins said, "Am I waiting for the next shoe to drop here, counselor?"

"Well, I did tell him about the affair between Boyd and his office manager—what was her name? Uh, oh, yeah. Alice Moore. 'The Merry Widow,' we called her. They worked a lot together and it was obvious to everybody that something was going on. The quick knowing smiles, the winks, the sly brushing of hands and all that. They were closer than just office stuff."

"Did Gilhooley get a statement from you?"

"Yeah, he recorded it. Kinda cute guy. Is he married?"

"I think so. By the way, Gail, why did you leave the firm?" Higgins touched all the bases, as he headed toward the end of his interview.

"That one's easy: look around Bob. Sunshine!"

"Yeah, I get it." But Higgins was torn. *Should I take her statement, too? It is against the interest of the client and, under the rules of discovery, it would have to be turned over to the prosecution. I could just let it lie and give Avery a report on what she said. On the other hand, Gilhooley already has her statement, so it's not like it will be a revelation.* He decided. "Now, can I take a recorded statement from you, too?"

Higgins steered the statement in such a manner that Gail Miller could only say that Boyd was *suspected* of infidelity—suspected and not confirmed with any real evidence. It was the best he could do under the circumstances.

Higgins waited around for the next flight back. He held the recorder to his ear, reviewing what he knew was a damning statement against his client, Boyd Richards.

CHAPTER
Twenty-Two

Imagination is a poor substitute for experience.
Havelock Ellis – English physician and social reformer

Wednesday, 11:15 a.m.

heila **Cummings was beside herself with glee.** She summoned Chief Worten and Gilhooley to her office. "Chief Worten, I told you if we arrested Richards back then, something would shake out. Sure enough, our star witness came along and with the forensics we needed. Can you even have imagined it? The blood they found is the same type as Callie's. I know... I know, it was too degraded for DNA, but so what? The witness hands us Boyd Richards with blood on his hands. What an image! How prophetic!" She then twisted in her chair and smiled. "Detective Gilhooley, you have topped off our case against Boyd

Richards by picking up on *his* affair. Put that all together and we have motive *and* the forensic evidence missing up till now. I am going to amend our complaint to murder-one." She sat back and rocked in her chair with a smug, satisfied expression. *I wonder what position Congressman Barrett has for me in D.C.?*

Worten sat quietly. He was thinking about Johnny Boy hanging there and Harlan Getz lying broken at the bottom of the stairs... and that damned alley. The news of Boyd's affair was important, of course; and the blood evidence was the lock the prosecutor needed for Boyd Richards' conviction. Still, there were those unanswered questions connecting the other two murders. He also knew Cummings would nix all that, given the chance, so he held his tongue. Chief Worten was troubled, because it was his duty to work for the prosecution, not the defense. But he also had a strong sense of right and wrong. He knew in an investigation, when something smells, you don't pass over it for personal or political reasons. He would continue the balancing act until the facts won out. *That damned alley!*

Assistant prosecutor Cummings dismissed Worten and Gilhooley and closed her office door before dialing. "It's going our way, Congressman. With this new forensic evidence, it looks like a slam-dunk." Sheila Cummings was doing her best not to sound giddy as she relayed the news to Congressman Bartlett.

"So far, so good, Ms. Cummings. My assistant has already informed me you are on your way to a conviction. I like that." He clicked off speaker phone and continued, "But be careful. Avery Reddy is a worthy opponent. He flirts with the jury and will be condescending toward you throughout the trial. And don't forget your law school warning: 'Jurors have minds of their own.'"

"Thank you for the advice. I will take it, and..."

"Good." Then came an abrupt click.

Sheila looked down into the phone, "And have a nice day to you, too!"

Chief Worten left a voice message: "Mack, meet me at Assante's ASAP. Important." The Mr. Assante pizza shop on Route 22 in Greenbrook, a staple for pizza lovers for decades, was a favorite of Mack's, and Worten knew it.

Two hours later the two friends were splitting a pie and catching up on things. "Mack, Cummings is beyond ridiculous. She really has it in for Richards. I admit, her case is getting stronger since the witness came forward with the blood evidence and, of course, there's the affair; but I am still troubled by the connection between the insurance company death and the tennis kid. And that freakin' alley. There's something very weird going on. Have you ever had a case go down two credible tracks at the same time? By the way, I haven't mentioned anything to her about it, but I think Gilhooley may have. If so, she's not going to trust anything I do or say."

"Sorry, you're in a tough spot, Bill. Tell you what. I'll take a shot at the insurance company. My side hasn't done that yet because Avery can't see wasting our time there. We're both working with our hands tied. I agree with you, there's something missing here. We know there's a connection between Johnny Boy and the insurance guy and that alley. We just haven't figured it out yet. The answer could be in that office. You forget, I spent a bunch of years doing insurance claims before I got my P.I. license."

Mack's phone buzzed; it was Avery. "Mack, you heard?"

"The blood and the affair, yeah. Bad breaks."

"I'll be sitting down with Boyd tonight. Gonna be tough. Any ideas?"

"Not yet, Avery. Not yet."

CHAPTER
Twenty-Three

Today is yesterday's pupil.

Thomas Fuller – English churchman and historian

Monday, early afternoon

*M*ack went up to the receptionist at the insurance company claims office and eventually met with manager Charles Howard. "I'd like to help you, Mr. Mackey, but we've cooperated with the police in every way possible. I don't see what a private detective is going to do here. It was a terrible accident, and our staff is still struggling with the shock of losing one of their own—and the way it happened..." He slowly shook his head as his voice trailed off.

"Mr. Howard, let me put it to you this way: what started out as an accident has turned into a murder, right here in your office.

I would think you would want to get to the bottom of it as soon as possible and not have your home office see you dragging your feet."

"Did you say *murder*?" Mr. Howard asked incredulously. "That young detective came by and poked around, but he never said anything about a murder. How could that be?"

Mack explained the medical examiner's findings to manager Howard and told him that the police are trained not to say much during an investigation. A look of deepening concern developing on Howard's face told Mack he was making progress.

His eyes blinking and with a stiffening of his back, Mr. Howard asked, "How can we help?"

"Well, to begin with, let me explain that I spent six years processing claims at Mutual Benevolent Risks after I left law enforcement, so I'm not exactly a babe in the woods here. I would think a good start would be to take a look at Mr. Getz's claims files and talk to the adjuster who has them now."

"I see. You are looking for a motive.'

"Very good. You're getting it." Mack felt cooperation building.

"Okay. That would be Alex DeFazio. He has Harlan's files now."

Mack sat Alex down in the small conference room and opened the conversation by saying, "Alex, what we have here is an exploratory mission. That is, you and I need to examine Harlan's files and see if there is anything that looks out of place—suspicious, okay? This is a murder case, so I really need your full attention."

Alex was enthusiastic. "Murder... wow! Sure, like, I'm all in, man." Then suddenly what Mack just said sunk in. "Wait a minute—Are you, like, saying Harlan was murdered?"

The two pored over Harlan's claims files for two full days, and a pattern began to emerge. It seemed that Harlan had an unbelievable talent for settling fairly large control claimant files, which Mack knew was not the norm. His own experience taught him that seriously injured parties were usually represented by lawyers, but not the case in too many of the Getz files. So, Alex and Mack put together a chart of the data with claimant names and addresses, along with statements made by those claimants. Dates that checks were written, dollar amounts paid, and copies of claim releases were all part of their research. At the end of day two, Mack pulled the plug.

"I think I have enough to go to the next step, Alex. Thanks for your help. Would you point me to your fax machine?" Mack thought, *This is the classic inside-outside insurance fraud. If you know your system and don't get greedy, it can go on a long time.*

He called his office on his way to the fax machine. "Nezzie, I'm faxing a list of names and addresses over. Get right on this. I need you to check out these people six ways to Sunday, got it?"

Nezzie's response was, "Humph!"

Mack smiled, dropped Nezzie and dialed Avery.

CHAPTER
Twenty-Four

Do what you can, with what you have, where you are.
Theodore Roosevelt – Former American president

"*I* don't care what you say, Avery, there's a connection here," Mack griped into his phone. Trying to explain his theory to the attorney, he went on. "How can you deny it? The insurance company murder is right down the alley from where Callie Richards' boy toy was strung up and made to look like a suicide. Even Bill Worten is on board here." As an afterthought, Mack said, "But don't let Sheila Cummings know that, for heaven's sake."

"Listen to me, Mack. I've told you before, my job is to concentrate on my case; not the Getz murder—if, indeed, it was a murder. For that matter, maybe the kid you say was murdered *was* really a suicide."

Frustrated, Mack persisted. "Okay. I guess I have to lay it out for you. The insurance adjuster and an outside guy were pulling off a scam. They stole many thousands of bucks from the company. I haven't figured out how big the fraud is yet, but it is big. I am sure there is a connecting motive with our case. If you won't go along with this, I'll do it on my own. Don't pay me for the hours I put in on that case."

"C'mon, Mack. You know me better than that." Avery softened. "I'm just playing my own tune here. Go ahead, but don't go too far off the reservation, please. I have to justify all this with Boyd."

"Thanks. My problem isn't proving the fraud; it's trying to identify the outside guy. He's gotta be the killer in the insurance company and maybe our case, too. I'll let you know."

Chief Worten's voicemail spewed the usual and Mack left a message: "Hello, Bill? See ya at Assante's ASAP. More good stuff." Mack hung up and began the drive back down U.S. 22 to Greenbrook and the pizza shop.

The two friends reviewed all that Mack had uncovered, passing papers back and forth. "You know, Mack, we might be able to get something going here with a hand-writing expert. That would be one way of proving all those claim releases were signed by the same guy. I think I can convince the state police guy to take a peek without setting up an official file on it yet."

"That's a good idea for starters. Higgins might be able to move that along, if you can't. While it won't tell us who he is, it would tie it up a little tighter. So, what do you think? A falling out among thieves? Good enough motive for murder?"

"Yeah, but too many loose ends."

CHAPTER
Twenty-Five

Someday each of us will be famous for fifteen minutes.
Andy Warhol – American pop artist

A Monday afternoon in December

Gordon Krone, formerly "Bruce," was enjoying his newfound notoriety. Assistant prosecutor Sheila Cummings wanted to have a dead-solid case against Boyd Richards, so she met with Gordon, herself. "Thanks so much for coming over, Mr. Krone. Your cooperation is much appreciated."

"No problem, Ms. Cummings. I consider it my civic duty to do whatever I can here. Do you think the case is going well?" Gordon had no intention of letting this play out on its own. *I need to know where her head is, and any way I can manipulate her, I will,* he thought. *Staying on top of this is my best chance of keeping myself off the hot seat—and putting Boyd Richards on it!*

Breaking every rule regarding the witness/prosecutor relationship, Sheila Cummings went over the entire case file with Gordon. Her passion for the case clouded her judgment. It did, however, afford her the emotional outlet she so desperately needed. She knew her future rested on a murder-one conviction, and that pressure was taking its toll.

"So, Mr. Krone, let's go over what will be *your* testimony again?"

Each time they did, Sheila made sure that Gordon used words and persuasion that explicitly characterized his ability to make the identification in the admittedly short time he encountered Richards at the 7-Eleven. She corrected him: "Gordon, it would be better if you used phrases like, 'No doubt in my mind.' Or maybe something along the lines of, 'It was obvious.' Please try to stay away from saying, 'I think so,' or anything that would convey weakness in your recollection. I have also found that juries can relate when a witness latches onto a comparative description. In other words, 'I remember thinking he looked just like my Uncle Jim.' Or something like that. Understand?"

Sheila knew she was crossing a line that she shouldn't cross. Prosecutors and defense lawyers often lead their witnesses to some degree, but they're not supposed to provide actual language beyond the witness's own thought processes, as Sheila had just done. She was at liberty to refresh the witness's recollection, but not to redirect his memory.

"You have to understand, Gordon, the defense will challenge your ability to make an identification based on such a quick inter-action as you describe—just bumping into each other for a few seconds. That's not going to be strong enough. Especially, since you admit you saw him on the news weeks later and could still say it was the same man. Understand?"

Gordon nodded his head, raised an index finger implying deep thought, then said, "How about this: 'When I came out of the men's room, I saw this man coming toward me. It was obvious he was upset, because of the look on his face. He was distressed. We both went in the same direction to avoid one another for a couple of back-and-forths, and I smiled; but he bumped into me, like, with no patience for me, and as he passed, I could clearly see blood on his hands and face. He was holding his hands up like this. His hands were only inches from my face. I'll never forget the look on his face!' How's that?"

"Now we're getting somewhere," said Sheila. "But you need to slow it down and allow me to jump in for a more dra-matic effect. We will keep on working on this, Gordon. You're doing great."

When Gordon Krone left the meeting, Sheila walked over to her office window, gazed out over the busy streets of the city and thought back to her law school days. Specifically, she zeroed in on an ethics class that warned young lawyers against being so caught up in winning their cases that they found themselves stretching the truth. She knew coaching Krone beyond his own memory was wrong, but, *What the hell, Avery will be doing the same, right?* Nevertheless, she knew she was on a slippery slope.

CHAPTER
Twenty-Six

Lawyers spend a great deal of time shoveling smoke.
Oliver Wendell Holmes, Jr. – Former Associate Justice, U.S.
Supreme Court

he months passed with no break in the case for the defense. The subsequent police discovery papers turned over to Avery showed photos of the 7-Eleven men's room with the blood specks in the grout, together with analysis affirming the same blood type as Callie's. Depositions of the Richards Law Firm employees added emphasis to Boyd's affair with the office manager. The Grace Harjes deposition persuasively demonstrated the motive for Boyd to kill his wife in a jealous rage. Above all, Gordon Krone's testimony linking the bloodstain evidence to the defendant was about as damning as a set of facts could be. As is the norm, Gordon was deposed by Avery.

The deposition went without a glitch. Sheila Cummings was delighted.

Attorney Avery Reddy understood how steep this mountain of evidence was and broached the subject of taking a plea with Boyd Richards. Boyd blew his top. He said he would rather spend his life in prison, an innocent man grieving for Callie, before he would cave in to false charges and made-up testimony. "Krone is a setup. I've never been in that 7-Eleven store in my life, and the blood fiction is off the wall." He added, "Barrett is in on this. I just feel it!

Day One, the trial begins

The Boyd Richards murder trial began on a dreary, wet January day. Not yet snow, but not quite sleet either, the cold precipitation stuck to everything. Necks were pulled in and heads hunched over, as spectators gathered for the trial. The dismal weather was well suited for the foreboding atmosphere of a man on trial for his life. In the week leading up to the event, all the local newspapers did their best to bring readers up to date with the latest legal wrangling. The editorial pages buzzed with speculation about the possible outcomes. Headlines read, "Can Defense Withstand Irrefutable Evidence?" "Will Boyd Richards Testify?" "Suburban Murder, Sex Scandal Trial Begins." NBC, CBS, CNN and FOX all got in on the act, each with legal experts spouting sage advice to both sides of the courtroom.

Avery Reddy, Boyd Richards and the twins were crammed into a small anteroom just a half-minute walk down the hall from Judge Sidney Frankel's courtroom. Mack waded through the hysteria of humanity lining every square inch of the hallways. The bailiff stood guard in front of Frankel's locked courtroom, dreading the flood of onlookers and press expected when the word to unlock and admit came. Anticipation was tangible.

Mack squeezed into the small closet of a room, just as Boyd kissed both kids on their way out. The ordinarily refined, uppity and in-charge lawyer-turned-defendant was visibly shaken, doing his best to keep it together. Defense attorney Avery Reddy was going over his notes on a yellow legal pad. He nodded hastily to Mack and returned to his notes. Then it began.

Following the bailiff's "Hear ye, hear ye, the court will come to order," Judge Frankel queried both counselors for any last-minute motions or comments. There were none, so he started the process of choosing the jury.

Sheila Cummings, dressed in a gray pants suit, used her pre-emptory challenges carefully. She wasn't going to waste one of those when she could come up with one for cause. She addressed a prospective juror: "Thank you for your service to the court, Mr. Atkins. I see that you list a divorce on your jury questionnaire. I don't wish to embarrass you, but these questions are important. How long ago were you divorced?"

When Atkins responded that it was five years prior and admitted that infidelity was an issue, Sheila dismissed the juror for cause. She didn't want anyone on the jury who might be sympathetic to the defendant. Of course, it could work the other way, too, but it was too volatile a subject with too many possibilities to predict which way a juror would sway. Avery Reddy bought into that theory, as well. Both lawyers astutely avoided jurors with questionable marriage issues. They dwelled on whether or not a potential juror had ever been a victim of a crime or whether a family member or friend had been through a criminal trial.

During a mid-morning break, Avery and Boyd stood just outside the courtroom. Boyd piped up, "What a slow pain-in-the ass this jury selection is." He was fidgeting, obviously feeling the stress.

Avery said, "I suppose it looks like that, but it's really important that the prosecution doesn't get their jury, and she feels the same about us. It's slow and painful, but we both get a chance to interview each juror about their prejudices and impressions. It works."

By the end of the day, the jury was impaneled, and Judge Frankel, after dismissing the new jury for the night, admonished the parties to be on time in the morning.

Day Two, 9:00 a.m.

Sheila Cummings conducted herself professionally, exuding an air of complete control, despite her quaking inner self. As prosecutor, she had the floor first and began her opening argument.

"Ladies and gentlemen, this is a first-degree murder case and, as such, your serious attention will be required. My job is to present the state's case. Mr. Reddy over here represents the defendant, and the judge will be answering questions of law. What I need you to do in this case is to stay on the facts. Someone's reputation, personal standing in the community, physical appearance, political party or anything else about them has nothing to do with the facts I will be presenting. I will show the who, the what, the where, the when, and, yes, even the why of Boyd Richards taking a knife and brutally plunging it into his wife's chest—time after time after time." Sheila closed in on the front rail of the jury box and violently mimicked the plunging of the knife, as she spoke. It was so effective, the jurors in the front row drew back in their seats. She went on, "The prosecution will present overwhelming and indisputable evidence, both forensic and testimonial, for your consideration. Once we have completed this trial, I am confident you will find Boyd Richards guilty of murder in the first degree. Thank you."

Prosecutor Raymond Lant, seated near the back of the courtroom, frowned and put his head down. He had taken in this smart, mature-for-her-years law school graduate and groomed her. He saw in her potential for a great legal career and, being the mentor-type that he was, pushed her along. Now she was prosecuting his friend. After a moment, he got up and tip-toed out, conflicted and saddened.

Avery Reddy was at his best in front of a jury. The first order of business was to make the jury sympathize with him. He played the underdog to the hilt, citing the state's ability to gather together tremendous forces, against which one had an uphill battle, to say the least. "Ms. Cummings says she has—what was it?—'overwhelming and indisputable evidence, blah, blah, blah.'" He smiled at the jury in an effort to win them over early on. "Well, since we haven't heard it yet, we can't judge it, can we? All I ask of you is to keep an open mind. Don't be fooled with razzmatazz and bluster." He turned tauntingly to Sheila. "Drama belongs on the stage, not in this courtroom." Turning back to the jury box, he continued, "We will show that Boyd Richards is an innocent man and that the evidence against him is circumstantial, and the state cannot and will not prove him guilty beyond a reasonable doubt. Why..." Avery's voice hesitated, as he walked over to the water-streaked window next to the jury box, "that so-called 'evidence' wouldn't convince an umbrella to come in out of the rain." Several jurors chuckled. Reddy added nothing. He just nodded slowly at them and sat down. But he thought to himself, *That was a good start when you don't have shit!*

Judge Frankel checked his watch and said, "I have to hear a couple of motions in my office, so we will adjourn until 1:30, at which time, Ms. Cummings, you may introduce your first witness." He then turned to the jury, explaining there will be interruptions from time to time, "…but we really will have a trial here." The jurors laughed. Judges do their best to ally themselves with jurors. Most try to maintain a friendly rapport with their juries.

CHAPTER
Twenty-Seven

A judge is a law student who marks his own examina-
tion papers.

H.L. Mencken – American journalist and satirist

Bob Higgins joined Avery, Mack and Boyd at a deli down the block from the courthouse. Avery opened the conversation, "Before any of you speak up, let us understand that Sheila will be unrelenting. She will object constantly, which will not necessarily hurt us. Each time, I will look over at the jury for sympathy. I will do everything I can to show her as unfair and pushy. All the while, I will be a solid and mature presence, never raising my voice—always the face of reason. That's all fluff, I know," Avery said, almost apologetically. "And, frankly, we have an uphill battle, what with this blood evidence at the 7-Eleven. Anything new on that, Mack?"

"I stopped over there, but drew a complete blank. No one else recalls Bloody Boyd, sorry, Boyd, and, as we know, they don't save the security tapes. Any suggestions?"

Higgins asked, "Mack, how is that other thing coming? Do we see any connections to the insurance company murder?"

Before Mack could speak, Avery jumped in, "Enough! I am trying this case, not that one. Let's stay focused here." Avery shook his head in disgust.

"Avery, there *is* a connection. That alley connects the insurance murder to Johnny Campbell and directly to Callie Richards. Why can't you see that?" Mack was adamant.

"Okay. Here's my problem: So far, the jury hasn't heard much about Johnny Boy. Maybe they haven't thought about him, either. At least, I hope not. Don't you see the quandary I am in? If I go your way and argue someone other than Boyd killed the insurance guy and Callie and Johnny Boy, I open the door for Sheila to suggest that Boyd had a motive for killing Johnny Boy. In the real world, Mack, he did have a motive. His wife was having an affair with the kid, for Christ's sake. They can't prove he killed Johnny Boy, and they don't have to; the suggestion will float out there and give the jury all the more reason to convict Boyd on Callie's murder. The insurance guy? Too confusing, so they'll gloss over it. Sheila knows Johnny Boy was a murder and not suicide. She can just as easily accuse Boyd of setting up the fake suicide as anyone else. She's hoping I open that door, and I'm not gonna do it!"

"Yeah," Mack said apologetically. "That's why you're the lawyer and we're the grunts. I never thought about it in that light. Guess we need to punch harder at our end. Sorry, Avery."

Avery waved it off.

Mack called his office. "Nezzie, I want you to go over all the police reports in the Richards file, as well as my and Bob's notes and put it into a timeline. We are looking for a pattern or something that pulls all this together. Any questions, call me."

"Okay, boss. I'm glad you called. I checked on all those names from the insurance company. Are you ready for a bombshell?"

"Go ahead."

"They're all dead! I checked restricted access, and every single one of them is pushing up daisies. I couldn't just give you that without doing some confirmation, so I went to Ancestry.com and more than half of them show up there—deader than doornails. I checked more and found that all of their names and stuff must have been taken from headstones in the same cemetery."

"Beautiful. It all fits. What about addresses?"

"Did that, too. Every address is some kind of mail service, like a UPS store. All fake."

"Luv ya, kid. Get that timeline going, ASAP!"

Nezzie hung up with a smug smile and spread everything she had for the timeline out on the conference table.

Trial resumed with Sheila calling Detective Gilhooley to the witness stand. He referred to his notes as his testimony was taken. He described the murder scene, characterized his interviews with witnesses and his interfacing with the medical examiner. Gilhooley had testified before, so he knew how to couch his answers to favor the prosecution. When he was done, a mental picture of the state's case was well under way.

Avery Reddy refrained from objecting to some of the hearsay stuff for a reason. He didn't want to start off with the jury as a whiner who bites on every point the prosecution makes. That would give the impression he feared the evidence. Oh, he did, but the jury couldn't know that.

"Detective, I see you are referring to your notes," Avery began. "As you so aptly explained in your testimony, this is a very serious case." Doing a heads-up motion to the jury, he continued, "Couldn't you have answered those questions without looking at notes?"

"Some of the details, such as times and dates, are important, so I make sure I have them right by looking at my notes." Gilhooley sat back, self-assured.

"Your honor, we would like to have a copy of this detective's notes," Avery said, glaring at Sheila, then back at the jury with an irritated face. "We were apparently denied this when we asked for all records." His play to the jury included raised eyebrows and a sour expression.

"Objection. Counsel knows it's normal for the police to refer to their notes, your honor. He has all the police reports he needs." Sheila knew Avery's reputation for charming juries. "He is grandstanding and we all know it."

"I see no reason why he cannot have the notes. Let's move on Mr. Reddy."

Avery finished up with Gilhooley without making any inroads, but he figured that would be the case. The police usually have their ducks in a row on the witness stand. *I know she's waiting for me to try and link the insurance guy and Johnny Boy to Callie... not goin' there, Sheila baby.* He smiled at Sheila, as he cozied into his chair. She looked away and then called her next witness.

"The prosecution calls Dr. Jacob Restin."

Once sworn in and qualified as an expert witness, Doc Restin went through his autopsy findings and the toxicology report. "The victim, Callie Richards, was a well-developed and well-nourished forty-two-year-old female in apparent good health. Her muscle tone suggested regular athletic activity. Analysis of her hair did not suggest any illegal drug usage. There was no drug residue found in her organs, as well. As to the method of death, she was stabbed in the chest multiple times. The cause of death was when a sharp instrument, probably a knife, sliced through her aorta resulting in almost immediate bleed-out and death. A trace of white wine was identified in her stomach contents along with some kind of cheesy pasta." The report droned on like that for half an hour.

"Your witness, Mr. Reddy."

"To your knowledge, Dr. Restin, was the murder weapon ever found?'

"I don't believe so, no. I say that because I was never given the opportunity to compare it to the wounds."

"Could you determine if the victim had engaged in sex recently?"

"No, there was no evidence indicating she had engaged in sex that day. I could not comment as to any other time period, however."

"Doctor, in your report you referred to shallow wounds and attached a meaning to them. Would you explain that to us?"

"As I say in my report, it appeared that the deep wound just below her sternum was the fatal blow. But there were another dozen shallow punctures in her upper chest, some of which slightly penetrated her rib cage but seemed to be added as an afterthought. They were tentative compared to what was apparently the first blow. In my experience, I see those additional strikes—weak as they are—as an attempt to make it look like this was a crime of out-of-control passion."

"How can you say that without being there and observing it?"

"Perhaps my representation of the motive would be more in the purview of the psychiatrist, not me. But I felt compelled to mention it, anyway. You see, the nature of a wound is directly related to not only with what, but how it is delivered. I deal with that type of analysis on a daily basis. In my judgment, those subsequent wounds appeared superfluous, added as an afterthought, if you will."

"So, as an expert witness, and just to be clear, you think the killer might have been someone trying to mislead the police investigation?"

Sheila, realizing Dr. Restin just admitted he was not a psychiatric expert and his comment as to possible motive for the shallow wounds went over the line, jumped to her feet. But before she could finish her objection, Dr. Restin leaned forward and said, "That's right."

"Objection sustained," said Judge Frankel, but the seed was sown. Avery planted the idea that the killer could be someone other than an insanely out-of-control Boyd Richards. The judge wasn't through. "Mr. Reddy, you will confine your cross-examination to facts, not suppositions. And you, Doctor, will not answer a question when there is an objection." Rotating to his left, he instructed, "The jury will disregard that last question and answer." Frowning back at Avery, he added, "Save that stuff for your closing argument. Is that fully understood?"

"Yes, Your Honor." Undaunted, Avery turned in the direction of the jury, with his back to the judge and the prosecutor, eyebrows bunched in a hurt expression this time. *My client and I are such victims!* Avery was good at this.

Sheila Cummings dropped back into her seat, thinking, *Win one, lose one—Isn't that what Raymond taught you about the point-score in a trial? Just keep focused, Sheila. Don't let slick Avery get to you. Focus.* She threw a quick glance at Avery. *Wait until my star pupil gets up there, smart ass!*

CHAPTER
Twenty-Eight

God save me from my friends — I can protect myself from my enemies.

Marshall de Villars – 18TH century French general

Day Two, late afternoon

"Your Honor, the prosecution calls Mrs. Grace Harjes** to the witness stand."

Nervous to her core, Grace rose and pushed through the gate and was sworn in. She stood straight and spoke with conviction.

"Please state your name and address," Sheila began.

"My name is Grace Mary Harjes, and I live at 204 Manor Hill Drive, Summit, New Jersey."

"Mrs. Harjes, what was your relationship to the decedent in this case?"

Narrowing her eyes into a hateful glare directed at Boyd Richards, she leaned forward and said, "She was my best friend. We were neighbors." Grace had recovered her mojo. And she bought into the theory that Boyd Richards killed Callie and was going to do her best to contribute to his conviction.

"Tell me, Mrs. Harjes, to your knowledge, was Callie Richards having an extramarital affair just before she was killed?"

"Yes, she was. It was with the tennis pro at our club. But she only did that because she knew Boyd was messing around with someone at his office and..."

Avery rose. "Objection. Hearsay, Your Honor, and please ask the witness to refrain from volunteering."

Sheila countered, "Your Honor, if you will allow me, I can show this is not hearsay and came directly from the decedent's mouth. That is, Callie's comments to Grace are an exception to the hearsay rule under Rule 804 of The New Jersey Rules of Evidence." Sheila had her law book open and read, "To quote that section exactly: *'trustworthy statement by a deceased declarant.'* Your Honor, this is specifically one of the enumerated exceptions." Sheila looked up expectantly at the judge.

"Okay, Ms. Cummings, I get it." The judge frowned and turned to Grace. "And the witness will limit her answers to the question asked and nothing more." The judge went back to his notes. He nodded for Sheila to continue.

Sheila continued, "Mrs. Harjes, was there a time when you had a conversation with Callie Richards wherein she expressed concern about her marriage and her husband's fidelity?"

"Yes, Callie told me she thought Boyd was cheating on her."

"Did she discuss why she thought that?"

"Your Honor," Avery was on his feet again. "Same objection. Since Mrs. Richards is not here to verify that conversation, and the nature of the testimony is important, how can we be assured of this witness's impartiality, as well as the accuracy of her testimony? And now we are to hear what the other party *thought?*"

Sheila wasn't yielding. "Your Honor, Mrs. Harjes's testimony is just part of the state's case. We will be offering another witness who will confirm that the defendant carried on an adulterous affair with a co-worker, which should give Your Honor reason to rule in my favor."

"More hearsay, Ms. Cummings?" Avery smirked at the jury.

"Actually, Mr. Reddy, it will be the person he had the affair with. Will that do?"

"Enough! Both of you will address the court, not each other. Overruled, for now, Mr. Reddy. You many continue, Ms. Cummings, but I am reserving my ruling on this."

"Thank you, Your Honor. Mrs. Harjes, the question was why Callie thought her husband was cheating on her."

Grace responded, "Callie was alone when the twins went off to college. Boyd became distant, and there were those phone calls with no one there. Boyd said he had to work on weekends. Callie thought that was strange, because he had never done that before. She just had strong feelings that Boyd was cheating."

"And it turns out, he was. Isn't that right? It's okay, don't answer. Your witness."

Avery got up with his yellow pad in hand. "Mrs. Harjes, you say you were Callie's best friend. Is that right?"

"Absolutely."

"Tell me, Mrs. Harjes, does a friend plant the seed of distrust in someone else's marriage? Does a friend then set up her friend with a young tennis pro to get back at her friend's husband, because she *thinks* he is cheating on her friend? Does a friend do those things, Mrs. Harjes?"

"Objection," Sheila shouted. "Your Honor, he can't harass the witness!"

"Your Honor, we can produce evidence that the entire testimony of this witness is based on innuendo with no basis in fact *at the time* the alleged conversation took place. But if you let her answer, I think it will resolve itself. I don't think the witness wants this dragged out."

The judge tapped his pen and peered over his glasses at Mrs. Harjes. "I don't usually engage witnesses in conversation, but is what Mr. Reddy said true?"

"Well, I did talk to Callie about it before we knew anything for sure. And I did introduce her to Johnny just to spite Boyd, but it did turn out he was cheating, so..."

"That will be enough." Judge Frankel sat straight up. "I will now rule on Mr. Reddy's objection: Since the conversation between Callie Richards and this witness was based on supposition and no evidence of infidelity *at that time*, I am ruling in favor of the defense." His Honor then instructed the jury: "The jury will ignore the testimony of this witness and place no value on it when you deliberate. I know this appears strange to you, but this happens in trials and it is a good thing."

"Thank you, Your Honor." Avery was outwardly pleased, but Sheila wasn't upset. The jury heard it, and that's what counted. Avery knew that, too.

Judge Frankel checked his watch and said, "It's getting late, so let's take this up tomorrow morning starting at ten. I have a couple more motions to dispose of before we get underway." He then turned to the jury and said. "The jury is excused for the night. As always, my admonition to you is that you do not discuss this case among yourselves or with anyone else until the end of the trial and during your deliberations. Court is adjourned."

CHAPTER
Twenty-Nine

He that flings dirt at another dirtieth himself.
Thomas Fuller - English churchman and historian

*I*t was early evening, and Sheila was holding her
own little court. Detective Gilhooley was helping
her line up witnesses for the coming trial days. Sheila celebrated
the headlines: The *Star Ledger* read, "Will Boyd Hopalong or
Be Corralled?" Then there was the *Courier News*, "Defense:
Reddy Whipped?" The *New York Post* posted, "Sex in Jersey
Suburbs? Ah Hah!"

Gilhooley laughed along with Sheila but said, "I don't get
the first one. What's with the Hopalong thing?"

Sheila laughed, "Yeah, I guess you never heard of William
Boyd, also known as Hopalong Cassidy, big cowboy star in the
forties and fifties. It's okay, Gilhooley, just get me my witnesses."

Sheila was pleased with the way the newspapers were portraying the trial. She knew that Congressman Barrett would be monitoring everything, as well.

Day Three begins

When trial resumed in the morning, Sheila called her next witness. "Your Honor, the prosecution calls Mrs. Alice Moore."

Boyd Richards, up to now, was doing his best to sit impassively, yet interested, as he conferred with Avery at the defense table. But when Alice's name was called, his shoulders slumped and he slowly shook his head in anguish.

After her swearing in, Alice Moore timidly sat in the witness chair, her hands folded in her lap. Her submissive facial expression conveyed utter defeat. In her late forties, and a widow, she was an attractive woman with mid-length brown hair and clear pale skin.

"Mrs. Moore, where are you employed, in what capacity, and for how long?"

In a quiet, demure voice, she replied, "I am office manager at the Boyd Richards law office. I have been so employed the past eleven years."

"Mrs. Moore, at any time during your employment at the Richards law firm did you and Boyd Richards enter into an extramarital affair?"

Mrs. Moore took a deep breath and held her chin up. "Yes."

"Please tell the court how it started."

Speaking in a soft, halting voice, she explained, "It was not intentional on either of our parts. It just... happened. We were working late on several large projects and we became close, I guess. I'm not sure I can explain it, really."

"Please tell us how long you were involved with the defendant."

"Not long, actually. We resisted it for the longest time. You see, my husband died several years before. Boyd and Callie were both very supportive of me during my difficult time and that kind of nurtured a deeper friendship. It didn't take much to go over the line." Alice then sat up straighter and said in a loud and more confident voice, "But it wasn't long before we realized it was crazy," she shook her head, "and we agreed to go back to... whatever." She looked at Boyd and blurted out, "I am so sorry. It was my fault, not yours!"

"Your Honor?" Sheila didn't have to spell it out.

"The witness will answer questions, not engage in any other discussion. Is that clear?"

"Sorry, but people have to know that."

"Enough!" The judge was losing his patience.

Sheila turned to Avery. "Your witness."

Avery rose and, sensing the drama of the moment, frowned for the benefit of the jury. He just stood there apparently pondering.

Finally, he said, "Your Honor, I see no reason to trouble this witness further. She is obviously distressed and I don't want to add to it. She has been forthright in her answers and made her point."

Judge Frankel slammed his hand down, "There you go again, Mr. Reddy. If you're going to testify, why don't you call yourself as a witness?"

"Sorry, Your Honor." Again, Avery squinted hurtfully at the jury as he returned to the defense table.

Avery whispered to Boyd, "That went well. Alice got more sympathy than I expected. Sheila will regret calling her."

Boyd replied, "She had to call her to get the affair in after Grace's testimony. I agree. It backfired, but poor Alice. She doesn't deserve this."

CHAPTER
Thirty

Thou shalt not bear false witness against thy neighbor.

God

Day Three continues

"*Y*our Honor, the prosecution calls Gordon Krone to the stand."

Avery muttered under his breath, "Here we go!"

After his swearing in, Gordon sat back in the witness chair, straightened his tie and wriggled himself into a comfortable position, his attention fixed on Cummings.

"Please state your full name, age and city in which you reside."

"I am Gordon Francis Krone. I am thirty-six years old and live in Union, New Jersey."

Sheila Cummings skillfully led Gordon through his testimony: his stop at the 7-Eleven, the bumping into Boyd Richards, his observation of the blood, and the defendant's attitude at the time. She even allowed him to get in his basic police training, as well as his prior employment as a corrections officer.

"Finally, Mr. Krone, is the man you saw in the 7-Eleven that day in the courtroom today?"

Gordon turned and pointed directly at Boyd Richards. "Yes, that's him, right there."

"Let the record show the witness pointed to the defendant. Your witness, Mr. Reddy." Sheila returned to her seat, satisfied that Gordon had followed her instructions perfectly.

Avery rose slowly, shaking his head from side to side. "I just don't see how all that time could go by—and in just a brief moment of contact—you could form such a solid recollection of the man you say you bumped into."

"Is there a question somewhere in there, Your Honor?" Sheila would protect her star witness.

"Ms. Cummings is right. Can we have a question, Mr. Reddy?"

Avery continued, "I'm getting there, Judge. Mr. Krone, let's go over this in microbursts. Know what I mean?"

"I think so. You mean like mini-second to mini-second?"

"Yes, that's it."

"Okay. Well, first I opened the door to leave the men's room and looked up."

"Good start." Avery wanted to interrupt as much as possible. His strategy was to keep the witness off balance.

"Then I saw this guy."

"Which guy?"

"I mean, the defendant. He was coming toward me in a hurry and…"

"How could you tell he was in a hurry?"

"He got close to me quickly. Really fast."

"Can you demonstrate how that happened to the court?"

Gordon answered quizzically, "I guess so."

Avery turned to the judge. "Your Honor, I would like this witness to demonstrate to the jury just how this alleged encounter took place. May we use the space in front of the tables here and maybe utilize the services of the bailiff to represent the man the witness bumped into?"

Sheila would have none of this. "Your Honor, this is ridiculous. They bumped into each other quickly, okay? That should be enough."

"No, Ms. Cummings. I think the jury should see this. Go ahead, Mr. Reddy. Bailiff?"

"Okay, Mr. Krone. Let's make believe this is the men's room door, over here. Please place the bailiff where you recall first seeing the man you bumped into."

Gordon played his part, as did the bailiff. Avery had them do it several times, and each time he counted off the seconds.

"Okay, Mr. Krone, you may resume the stand. As the jury saw and heard, the average time it took to complete this encounter was four seconds. I think we all agree with that."

"He's testifying again, Judge." Sheila was livid.

"Sorry, Your Honor. I'm just trying to move this along." Avery walked up and stood very close to Gordon on the witness stand. "Interesting," he said jokingly. "You must have exceptional observational powers to be able to put all that together in just four seconds. I mean, the identification, the blood, the bump—all in four seconds?"

"Your Honor, when is this going to stop?" Sheila was unraveling.

Avery raised his hand in surrender, as he walked back to the defense table. "No further questions of this witness."

"The prosecution calls William Brooks to the stand." After the witness was sworn in, Sheila began her questioning. "Mr. Brooks, by whom are you employed and in what capacity?"

"I am a forensic serologist with the New Jersey State Police Laboratory in West Trenton. I have been so employed for the past sixteen years."

"Mr. Brooks, did you have occasion to examine blood evidence in this case?"

"Yes, the samples were submitted by the Union County Prosecutor's Office, and all proper signatures, dates, and handling explanations as to the chain of evidence were in order."

"Did you personally do the analysis of the blood submitted, and, if so, what were your conclusions?"

"Yes, I did. While the blood evidence submitted was degraded somewhat, I was able to determine that the blood type was O-positive, that of the deceased in this case."

"So, for the benefit of the jury; the blood found on the men's room floor in the 7-Eleven was the same blood type as the deceased, Callie Richards?"

"That's correct."

Your witness, Mr. Reddy.

Avery was on the hunt. He rose and came around the defense table, moving with a sense of urgency. He disdainfully said, "Oh, that's really damning evidence, isn't it, Mr. Brooks? I mean, are you saying that was Callie Richards's blood?" Avery was, for the first time in the trial, aggressively pushing a witness and making sure the jury got his point.

"No, I am not saying that. I am saying it was the same blood type."

"Weren't you able to do a DNA analysis? That would have revealed a lot, no?"

"As I said, the blood evidence submitted was degraded, so DNA was out of the question."

"No DNA?"

"No DNA."

"So," Avery continued, "all you can say is that the blood taken from a men's room floor is blood type O-positive, right?"

"That's why I am here testifying, Mr. Reddy," Brooks answered with a tinge of annoyance.

"Mr. Brooks, how do the various blood types break down over the population of the United States?"

Brooks considered the question for a moment, then confidently replied, "The approximate distribution of blood types in the U.S. population is as follows: O-positive: 38 percent; O-negative: 7 percent; A-positive: 34 percent."

"Okay, so would you agree if I told you 38 percent—that's the O-positive—of a population of three-hundred-twenty million people would be one-hundred-twenty-one million?"

"Let me check... just one moment." Brooks reached into his pocket and pulled out a palm calculator. The court room was quiet while he poked away at the gadget, then, satisfied with his computation, he answered, "That is correct, Mr. Reddy."

"So then, the blood traces found on the men's room floor could've been left there by any one of one hundred twenty-one million other people. Isn't that what you are testifying to today?"

"I suppose so."

"No further questions of this witness." Avery had made his point.

Sheila, on redirect, asked, "Mr. Brooks, just to be clear, the blood *was* the same blood type as Callie Richards?"

"Yes, that's all my testimony is intended to show, Ms. Cummings, because I was not able to conduct adequate DNA testing due to the condition of the evidence submitted."

"Your Honor, at this point the prosecution's case rests." Sheila exuded confidence.

The judge summoned both attorneys to a sidebar conversation. "Mr. Reddy, how many witnesses do you anticipate and how much time involved?"

"At this moment, Judge, I am not sure. I have half a dozen character witnesses lined up, so it could take a couple of days."

"Okay, let's wrap up for today." Judge Frankel waited until both lawyers were back to their tables, then announced, "That will be all for today. Back here at 9:00 a.m. tomorrow, and the defense will enter its case. Again, I caution the jury to refrain from discussing the case. Court is adjourned."

CHAPTER
Thirty-One

All our reasoning ends in surrender to feeling.
Blaise Pascal – French physicist and Christian philosopher

hat evening Boyd and Avery met at Avery's office in Westfield. Boyd was upbeat. "I thought you did well, Avery. You took Grace Harjes apart. Mrs. Moore didn't hurt that much, and the serologist's testimony was blunted. And that guy, Krone—you demonstrated how quick that interaction was. So far, so good."

"I'm not so sure," countered Avery. "Cummings got in her points, leaving me to play catch-up. That Gordon Krone was a super witness for the prosecution. Sure, I raised some doubt; but if you were a juror, what would you think? The defendant had an affair, so did his wife. The defendant can't say where he was when his wife was killed. Someone saw him with blood on his hands in a 7-Eleven. Then blood, the same type as his wife's, was found in that very same men's room. I don't like it at all."

"Surely, Avery, you don't think we're in trouble," Boyd said, a deep frown developing.

"Boyd, stop thinking like a lawyer and start thinking like a plumber or a salesman or a schoolteacher, because that's who's on our jury. And your future will shortly be in their hands!"

"In that case, I have to testify."

"No. Cummings will skewer you. She will throw damned-if-you-do, damned-if-you- don't questions at you. She will put you on the defensive, which is not where you want to be. No, Boyd, that would be a big mistake. I can't allow it."

"Avery, this is my life on the line, here. If I can't get them to believe in me, it will be my own fault. I've given this a lot of thought. Even if we win, I lose. My reputation will be shot in any event. If we win, I will be the rich lawyer politician who got away with murder. We need to do more than just getting me off, Avery. You must put me on the stand and let me talk to the hearts of the jury. Please!"

"So help me, Boyd, if you come across with that arrogant lawyer attitude, you will be cooking your own goose!"

CHAPTER
Thirty-Two

*It takes two to speak the truth—one to speak, and
another to hear.*

Henry David Thoreau – 19th century philosopher

Day Four begins

"Your Honor, the defense is ready to proceed."

Avery put the testimony of five character witnesses into the record, and Sheila asked not a single question of them. She just sat listening stone-faced.

"At this time, Your Honor, the defense calls Boyd Richards to the stand." Avery had reluctantly acceded to Boyd's demand to testify. A murmur flowed through the courtroom, and several jurors exchanged surprised glances. Even the bailiff looked up, his usual boredom with courtroom banter suspended. Sheila

Cummings, with an elevated brow, nodded her head at Avery, a challenge with a sprinkle of admiration.

"Very well, Mr. Reddy. Proceed." The judge inched forward in his chair. He was eager to hear this, too.

Boyd rose and walked the ten feet to the witness stand. He answered, "Yes, I do!" in a loud and emphatic voice to the court clerk's swearing-in speech. The stately looking, successful lawyer-turned-defendant calmly took the witness stand and looked directly at his attorney. He sat erect with his head up.

Avery got up close to Boyd, leaning on the railing, yet facing the jury. He got the obvious question out of the way first, "Mr. Richards, did you kill your wife?"

"I did not! I loved her dearly. I am still in shock all these months that she is gone. I have not had a chance to grieve." Boyd was clearly on offense. Speaking slowly, he was following Avery's advice: "Project a blend of indignation and humility; and for heaven's sake leave your lawyerly arrogance at the door."

Avery picked up the pace. "During this trial, we have heard of your marital infidelity, as well as that of your wife. Please address these matters." The two had decided that they would attack these issues head-on. Avery would set up the topic, and Boyd would express himself as best he could.

"It is true that Mrs. Moore and I behaved improperly, and for that we are both deeply sorry. Just as she said, I, too, am not sure how it happened. The best I can say is that we were working on an important project after hours and became so wrapped up in the minutiae that we lost sight of everything around us. One night we just... I don't know... fell into each other's arms. Not long afterwards, we had a serious talk. We understood it had to end, so we resolved to do just that. All of this is, regretfully, true; but we ended it after just a few weeks and that was at least six months before... Callie's death. I still have a hard time saying that... 'Callie's death.'" Boyd shook his head and blinked his eyes in disbelief. He was persuasive.

"Please cover the circumstance of your wife's infidelity with the tennis pro."

"To this day, I am still in disbelief. I had no idea of an affair on her part. In fact, the first I heard of it was when we opened the discovery package from the prosecutor in your office. I can hardly believe it to be true." He turned to face the jury. "If you knew my wife, you would never think her capable of that type of behavior. She was patient, loving and..." He choked up and could not finish the sentence. After a few seconds composing himself, he went on, but with a more unforgiving tone. "Now that I know it was Grace Harjes pulling the strings, it becomes more believable. She and Dan had marital problems, and Grace had no inhibitions when it came to having everyone know about it. She bragged about it, for crying out loud. Now, put that together with the fact that Callie had a get-along, go-along personality— that is, she was easily influenced by friends—it becomes more believable. I wish I had spent more time at home. I do recall telling Callie that I had to work some nights and weekends; but, as happens I suppose in most marriages, we don't always listen as well as we should. If Callie had an affair, I put that on Grace Harjes. She was always a bad influence. I'm rambling... I'm sorry."

Avery Reddy, defense attorney at his best, walked right up to the jury rail and continued questioning Boyd while searching the faces of the jury. "So, you ended your affair with Mrs. Moore six months before Callie's death. You did not know of Callie's infidelity with the tennis pro. You loved your wife and had no reason to do her harm. Let me repeat that last part: No reason to do her harm. Is all that precisely correct, Mr. Richards?"

Boyd leaned forward, on the verge of tears, toward the jury and in a pleading voice said, "Yes... Yes."

"Your witness, Ms. Cummings." Avery was satisfied with his client's testimony, but he knew the worst was yet to come. *The fox is in the hen house, and Boyd Richards is about to get his feathers ruffled!*

CHAPTER
Thirty-Three

This is a court of law, young man, not a court of justice.
Oliver Wendell Holmes, Jr. – Former Associate Justice of
U.S. Supreme Court

heila **Cummings was out for blood.** She headed toward the witness chair with her head down, on a mission. "Mr. Richards, how touching! Your little soliloquies were heart wrenching. If only there was a scintilla of truth to them." She turned to half-risen about-to-object Avery and said, "I know, I know, a question. Comin' up."

She leaned on the railing in front of Boyd and studied the jury for a few seconds. "Mr. Richards, are you familiar with the saying, "'If it looks like a duck, walks like a duck, and quacks like a duck, it's a duck?'" Richards didn't bite. Avery started to rise but thought better of it. *Maybe she'll go too far and make a fool out of herself.*

Sheila looked at Boyd and angled her head to the side, really expecting an answer.

Disdainfully, Boyd responded, "Is that part of your cross-examination, Ms. Cummings? If it is, you're asking me to take part in silly parlor games. I am not here to do that."

"Judge, please ask the witness to answer." Sheila was on a flight of haughtiness.

"Ask a question and I will, Ms. Cummings. I'm not here for any games, either." Judge Frankel's patience was wearing. He was tapping his pen, an indicator the judge was nearing his tolerance for tom foolery.

"Okay then, let's get to it. Look at this jury, Mr. Richards. Do you really expect them to believe that your affair with Mrs. Moore was as... as... what's the word? ...*innocent* as you made it out to be?"

"Innocent? No. I never said that."

"Wouldn't you say this jury could believe it was a motive for killing your wife?"

"Perhaps you will succeed in making them think that, Ms. Cummings; but it wasn't. We ended that half-a-year before Callie..."

"Oh, yes. So you say. But there's no way to prove that, is there?"

Boyd thought a moment. "No, I suppose not. It's kind of hard to prove the negative."

"Then there's that pesky blood on the 7-Eleven men's-room floor and the witness who saw you there—by the way, in distress and in a hurry. Any answer for that one?"

Avery stood. "Your Honor, does she get to have two closings? Could we have questions of the witness that are lawyerly and probative?" He was giving Boyd the time to put together an answer.

"Mr. Reddy, you put him on the stand. You put up with whatever comes." However, the judge did turn to Sheila and warned, "But within reason."

"Mr. Richards?" Sheila repeated.

"All I can say about that is the man is mistaken. I have never been in that 7-Eleven in my life. But let's think about this a moment." Boyd turned toward the jury. "If I had done this terrible thing—and in my own backyard—wouldn't I have used my own resources to clean up? There was the hose right near the pool. The downstairs bathroom was just steps away. It doesn't make sense." He turned back to Sheila. "There's no walking, quacking duck there, Ms. Cummings."

Undeterred, Sheila smiled and dropped her gaze to the floor. Angling her head to the side, she shot back, "Ever get upset, Mr. Richards? Ever lose control and do something stupid? Ever find yourself doing something one way, then realizing you could've done it better?

Avery, again trying to give Boyd time to react, complained, "Your Honor, could we have one question at a time? I object to counsel's machine-gun tactics!"

"Ms. Cummings?" The judge half-smiled at the machine-gun reference.

"Take any one and answer, Mr. Richards." Sheila was doing her own theatrical show.

Boyd thought a second, then answered, "Not that I can recall, Ms. Cummings. I'm only a methodic, dull, studious corporate lawyer. I don't think I have ever found myself in any of those circumstances you describe."

"Exactly!" Sheila got the answer she wanted. "Given the circumstances in the backyard next to the pool, the first time something like I posed happened—that is, stabbing your wife to death—there's no accounting for how you would act afterwards, is there? It's not unreasonable for your reason to go out the window and for you to panic, right?"

"Since I didn't do what you are talking about, I have no answer to that."

"You didn't have an answer when asked where you were at the time Callie was killed, did you? Oh, wait, you said you were in the law library; but no one saw you there, right?"

"That appears to be the case."

"Then there's Callie's infidelity. You didn't like that, did you?"

Not able to conceal his discomfort with that question, Boyd squirmed a little and muttered, "I knew nothing about that until after I was arrested."

"So you say. Another tough one to explain, huh? Wouldn't you agree that would be motive?"

He'd just about had it with her abuse: "No, I don't. If that were the case, Ms. Cummings, homicide squads all across the country would be overwhelmed with spouses killing each other, and marriage counselors would be out of work." Boyd's answer bordered on that arrogant lawyer image that Avery wanted kept out, yet several jurors did chuckle silently. One even poked the guy next to him in the ribs.

"Cute answer, Mr. Richards, but empty. In your case, you had your own affair and Callie had hers. And hers *really* bothered you, so you stabbed her to death. Mr. Richards, you killed your wife, and we all know it. No further questions." She left Boyd Richards shaking his head.

"If there is no redirect..." the judge probed Avery with a look that received a negative head shake back, "you may step down, Mr. Richards. I think we'll adjourn until tomorrow at 10:00 a.m. when summations will be heard." Judge Frankel rose after dismissing the jury with his usual warnings.

They had dinner at Europa Restaurant on Westfield Avenue in Elizabeth and went over the day's testimony. After ordering drinks and food, Avery kicked it off. "I think, all things considered, we did okay today. Not perfect, but okay. You held together well on the stand, Boyd. It wasn't easy with Sheila in full combat mode. I give you credit."

"Actually, I wasn't concerned about her. It's the looks on the juror's faces that keeps me guessing. What are they thinking, Avery? Like you said, they're plumbers, teachers, and such. I'm sure none of them has ever been confronted with such responsibility before."

"That's the beauty of the criminal justice system, Boyd. Juries consist of everyday people who do their best to sift through the evidence and come up with a just verdict. I grant you, it doesn't always happen, but most of the time it works. Each juror brings his own life experience, sense of morality, and even prejudices into the deliberation room. But, thankfully, it isn't up to one; it's up to the collaboration of all to come up with the final decision. I love it. I love the challenge before me each time I get up to persuade, cajole, and even embarrass them into *my* verdict. That's criminal law, Boyd."

Boyd shook his head. "You can have it! Give me an environmentally flawed oil lease or a tangled-up merger any day over this crap. I don't know how you do it—much too emotional. And, if you'll pardon the personal jab, just a little too much bullshit."

Avery laughed and brought them back to the case at hand. "Tomorrow, I go first. My summation will go through all the prosecution's evidence and diminish its importance, value and believability. Sure, I will do a little song and dance. They expect that, but the real meat is in the believability: 'Do you really think this man could commit this crime? He's a bookworm—a corporate lawyer who wouldn't know the first thing about creeping up behind someone and stabbing them to death.' I will be anticipating Sheila's comments and will try to blunt them before she gets to say them. I'm not finished with it yet; I'll be polishing it up till after midnight, so let's not stay here too late."

CHAPTER
Thirty-Four

The object of oratory alone is not truth, but persuasion.

**Thomas Babington Macaulay – British historian
and Whig politician**

Day Five, 10:06 a.m.

*T*he jury filed into the courtroom. Friendly conversations
they were having tapered off as they crossed the threshold
and took their seats. The jury had become a cohesive body in
its own comfort zone. Both Avery and Sheila were already at
their tables with piles of notes and legal pads placed strategi-
cally. Testimony and arguments hashed out, the trial was moving
to a different level, summations: where persuasion trumps fact,
where anything goes, where trial lawyers earn their keep.

Judge Frankel appeared almost cheerful this morning. He explained to the jurors that while the prosecutor went first and the defense second at the opening of the trial; the reverse takes place at the end. "The defense will address you first and will argue why you should acquit the defendant. The prosecutor gets the last word this time, and tells you why you should convict. It's that simple. But I want you to listen carefully to each of them, because you will need their arguments to assist you later on when you go into deliberations. During summations, there are no objections. Counsel gets to say pretty much whatever he or she wants to say to persuade you one way or the other. All I ask is that you pay attention to each of them."

"Mr. Reddy, you may begin."

Avery rose and approached the jury box deliberately. "Thank you, Your Honor. Ladies and gentlemen of the jury, you have heard Ms. Cummings and me sort of dueling it out over the past week or so. That's why they call it a trial." He paused, "It is *trying*, isn't it? All that arguing between supposed grownups." The silver tongue was at it again. Most members of the jury either smiled or snickered. "And both of us appreciate your patience. Now we are at the point in this trial where we go over the evidence and try to make some sense of it together."

Avery paced methodically back and forth in front of the jury box. He understood that what the jury *sees* during the summation is as important as what they *hear*. As he made each point, he paused and looked at the jury, as if cementing that particular argument into their minds. Hopefully a juror would think, *That pause must be important, because he stopped to look at me.*

"Let's cut to the chase. My client is charged with viciously, coldly and with malice aforethought taking a sharp instrument and plunging it into his wife's chest. As presented by the medical examiner, the perpetrator carried out this act from behind and above her while she was seated in a pool lounge chair. In other words, with *stealth*! I ask you to consider this: Would a husband have to sneak up behind his wife to get close enough to kill her. Wouldn't that be the necessity of a stranger? Here's some more food for thought: Ms. Cummings seems all worked up over the affair with Mrs. Moore and is hanging her 'motive hat' on that. Okay, let's examine it closer. My client says they ended their relationship six months before the murder, yet cannot prove the negative. Well, let's put it another way: Has Ms. Cummings proven the affair was going on up until the death of Callie Richards? She cannot and has not. Why? Because she can't prove her positive on that point. Where are those witnesses? They don't exist, because the affair was over half a year before. While we're on that subject, where's the witness suggesting that Boyd Richards knew his wife was having an affair? Same thing." Avery was in his element.

"You saw that it took an average of four seconds for witness Gordon Krone to make the supposed identification of my client at that 7-Eleven store. Not only that, it wasn't until almost seven weeks later that he saw my client on television being arrested to realize—in his mind—that it was the same person he bumped into. Given those facts, do you really think he could say with such certainty that was the man he saw? Obviously, it was someone else. Not my client. Oh, you say, 'What about the blood traces?' One in one-hundred-twenty-million? Please, spare me! They couldn't come up with DNA, so they took their shot with much lesser evidence. Hey, it's good old forensic evidence, so it must be gospel." Avery spoke that last sentence mockingly. "But, as it happens, Ms. Cummings asked a question of my client resulting in his answer that puts this whole thing at the 7-Eleven to bed. Why didn't he clean up at home, where everything was familiar and available to him? The alternative defies logic." Now Avery was leaning on the jury rail, getting right up close to some of the jurors in front to continue his pitch.

"There will soon come a time in this trial when the judge charges the jury. That is, he will be instructing you how to evaluate the evidence and to do so within the law. An important part of those instructions will cover the subject of reasonable doubt. You see, my client entered this courtroom an innocent man— until proven guilty beyond a reasonable doubt. In this case, I firmly believe that the hurdle of reasonable doubt has not been overcome by the prosecution.

"My friends, this is what we in the criminal defense bar call 'circumstantial pile-on.' But you are smarter than to fall for innuendo and poor evidence. I want to leave you with something else to include in your deliberations: Voltaire, a famous French writer, philosopher and historian, said, 'Common sense is not so common.' I want to believe that there is a great deal of common sense among you, members of our jury. Please exercise that common sense as you deliberate this case. Each time you are faced with a tough choice, ask yourself, 'Does this make sense?' To me, it makes no sense at all that Boyd Richards would take that sharp instrument, creep up on his wife from behind and stab her, then go and wash up in a 7-Eleven. We don't know who killed Callie Richards yet, but we will, I assure you." Avery stared at each of them for a long moment, nodding his head, then slowly walked back to the defense table and sat.

Judge Frankel nodded to Sheila. "Ms. Cummings?"

Sheila wasted no time getting over to the jury box. She left her notes on the prosecution table in order to show the jury she had her argument down cold. "Ladies and gentlemen of the jury, I come to you with a plea for common sense, as well. Only the common sense I speak of encompasses a totality of the facts, not just what Mr. Reddy wants you to consider. I believe this whole case comes down to the basics: means, motive, and opportunity. These are the bastions of criminal law. Question: Did the defendant have the means, the motive and the opportunity to brutally take the life of Callie Richards? Of the three, two are obvious: means and opportunity. He is a tall, healthy male easily equipped with the physicality to carry out the attack, so *means* is covered. As to *opportunity*, it happened poolside in his own backyard. We are left with *motive*. The defendant and his paramour admitted to their affair right here in court." She waved her hand over the courtroom. "So, that's a matter of record, right? Not only that, we've learned that Callie Richards was having an affair of her own. Plenty of motive to go around, right? But let's discuss motive a little more. You heard Detective Gilhooley testify. Did the police find anything missing from the home? Jewelry? Money? The family art collection? No, they did not. So, this was not a robbery or burglary gone bad, was it? No, it wasn't. The attack on Callie Richards was deliberate and vicious, and that very same common sense Mr. Avery alludes to tells us no one but the defendant could have or would have done it. I ask you: Who else *could* or *would* have done this? Sheila's eyes narrowed, as she walked back toward the defense table and pointed at Boyd. "No one else, just Boyd Richards, the defendant." She went on, "That common sense that Mr. Reddy so eloquently lectured us on falls short when it comes to motive, doesn't it? Yes, it does." Sheila was using the classic prosecutorial question-and-answer tactic with the jury, hoping it would last into their deliberations.

Sheila smiled and looked directly into the eyes of the first juror. "Surely, you recall the testimony of Gordon Krone." She moved to the next juror. "He was positive he saw the defendant at the 7-Eleven store." On to the next juror. "'Blood on his hands and face,' he said." Next one. "'In distress and in a hurry,' he said." Then, backing up slightly, she addressed the whole jury. "That blood... that blood, the same type as Callie's. It was her way of letting us know what happened here. There it is, wrapped up in a tight bow for you. I know you will do the right thing: That is, find, beyond a reasonable doubt, that Boyd Richards is guilty of murder in the first degree!

CHAPTER
Thirty-Five

A jury consists of twelve persons chosen to decide
who has the best lawyer.
Robert Frost – American poet

Same day, 11:15 a.m.

*J*udge **Sidney Frankel referred to his notes** as he began to charge the jury. "Members of the jury, now is the time for me to instruct you about the law you must follow in deciding this case. I will be explaining your duties and some general rules. I will give you the elements of the crimes charged in this case, as well as the essential ingredients of proof of those crimes."

The judge went on with his standard charge to the jury, spending a significant amount of time on the definition of "reasonable doubt." He explained how—should they find the defendant guilty—they might distinguish between murder in the first degree and the lesser—second degree. He also explained that the punishment was not their responsibility; rather, it was that of the judge, should there be a guilty verdict.

Both Sheila Cummings and Avery Reddy listened intently to the judge's charge, as there is always a chance that the judge might influence the jury with a word or phrase—however unintentionally. The chance of that happening, though slim, has resulted in over-throwing convictions in the past.

Finally, the judge covered the requirement of a unanimous verdict. "Your verdict, whether it is guilty or not guilty, must be unanimous. This means that to find the defendant guilty, every one of you must agree that the government has overcome the presumption of innocence with evidence that proves his guilt beyond a reasonable doubt. And to find the defendant not guilty, every one of you must agree that the government has failed to convince you beyond a reasonable doubt. Either way, your verdict must be unanimous."

With that, the jury was sent off to deliberate Boyd Richards's fate.

CHAPTER
Thirty-Six

Don't get mad, get even.

Robert F. Kennedy – American politician

*M*ack and his partner, Bob Higgins, followed the trial from a distance, while going about the business of private investigations on other cases. This morning they were following an insurance claimant whose injury allegations seemed blown out of proportion—according to the insurance company that hired them.

"He's making a right," warned Higgins over their Motorola two-way portable system.

"I see it. I'll pass by, you stick with him, and I'll pick him up on the next block."

"You got it." Higgins tailed the insurance claimant another couple of blocks, then turned into a bank parking lot once he saw

Mack's surveillance van come out of another lot and in behind the subject. They followed their man this way, by leapfrogging as they went. At no time could the subject see the same vehicle behind him for any length of time. They also screened themselves behind other vehicles where possible.

"He's turning into... I think it's a coffee shop or something," Higgins cautioned. "I'll pass by. He can only make a right out of here."

"Okay, I'll set up back here and catch some video when he comes out. He's walking without that limp. Don't know if you noticed."

"Yeah, saw it."

Mack's cell phone buzzed, the screen showing his office calling. Irritated, he thought, *Not now, Nezzie, we're on a surveillance. You know better!* He spoke sharply into the phone. "Okay, what's so important it can't wait until we're off this job, Nezzie?"

"Mack, this is bad. I'm sorry, but I know you'd want me to…"

"What's wrong?" Mack braced himself.

"It's Penny. She's in intensive care at Morristown Memorial."

"How bad?"

"Don't know yet. She had your office number in her phone under 'ICE,' you know—in case of emergency. The hospital front office wouldn't say anything more. I remembered you told me she was a nurse there, so I called the ER, figuring they would be more helpful. I guess she told them about you, too, 'cause one of the nurses let me know it was a head injury. She was apparently attacked in the parking lot when she reported for duty last night. I'm so sorry. How can I help, Mack?"

"Thanks, Nezzie. I'm on my way there. We'll stay in touch." Mack handed off the surveillance to Bob and roared off for the hospital. *Please, God, not again!*

He hated hospitals. Their cold polished floors and hallways, the all-too-officious attitude and intellectual superiority of the staff, and that antiseptic smell following you everywhere. Walking past the security post and into the ER brought back all the times he spent here with his Margie. *Please God, not again!*

"You cannot go in any farther. Can I help you, sir?" The young nurse was standing her ground in front of Mack. She was short and chubby and definitely in charge.

"I'm sorry. I'm here about Penny Lund. You know her? She works here."

"You must be Mack."

"Yeah, how is she?"

"She's gonna be okay. She took a nasty hit to the occipital area with something hard. It knocked her out. Right now, she's under observation in ICU. The doctors are worried about her brain swelling, but that hasn't happened yet."

"Anybody know how it happened?"

"I heard that the security guard in the parking lot saw it happen and got to her right away. His name is Gus, a retired cop, I think. He's off duty now."

Mack put Nezzie on identifying Gus, so he could talk to him later. In the meantime, he used the young nurse's influence to get him into the ICU for a few minutes. He was only able to view Penny through the glass. She was asleep, her head tilted to the left and covered in a skull cap of bandages, lumpier on the right side. An intravenous tree held a bottle dripping something into her left arm. An EEG monitor pulsed nearby with its thin line of brain waves flowing steadily from left to right. Mack felt anger welling up inside. He began to breathe hard with teeth gritted. He turned to the young nurse. "Thanks for letting me come up here. I'm sorry, I didn't get your name."

"Oh, sorry, I'm Judy."

"Judy, here's my card. Would you call me the minute she wakes? I want her to know I was here for her."

"Oh, we all know that. You're 'Mack the Dragon Slayer.'"

"Yeah, and one more to go!"

As Mack threaded his way through the sterile hospital halls back to the ER, he checked in with Nezzie. She reported, "I got the lowdown from the Morris Township PD, Mack. It's Gus Pendleton you want to talk to. He lives in Mt. Olive Township, but is probably asleep now. He worked the graveyard last night. I'll text you his address and phone number."

"Did I call you a peach yet this week?"

"Yeah, twice."

Just as Mack emerged from the ER, he met Brenda Higgins coming in.

A worried look on her face, she asked, "How is she, Mack?"

"Don't know yet. She's in ICU. How did you get here so fast? And how did you know?"

"I was at the mall when Bob called me. I'll stay here a while, but will they let me in?"

"Talk to Judy, a nurse in the ER. She will keep us posted. Thanks, Brenda, you're a peach, too. I have something to attend to, but I'll be back later. If she wakes up..."

"You'll be the first to know." Brenda headed off to the ER.

Mack pulled the address for Gus Pendleton off his cell phone and drove backroads to the Flanders area of Mt. Olive Township and Pendleton's small Cape Cod home. An elderly woman was tending to a vegetable garden off to the side of the driveway. She looked up suspiciously when Mack drove in. She lifted the shovel, as she stood up. "Who are you and what are you doin' in my driveway?"

Mack got out and with his hands half-up and palms out in front signaling "no problem." He smiled and said, "If you're Mrs. Pendleton, I'm here to speak to Gus about the nurse who was attacked last night. I'm sure he must've mentioned it. Oh, and by the way, I was 'on the job,' too."

Mrs. Pendleton eased up with the shovel and the attitude. She said her husband would be back shortly. "He sleeps later in the day, just before he goes back in for his midnight shift. All through his police days, he preferred the night shift. So, when he retired from East Orange, he got a job that offered him the same. We both got used to it, you know?"

Mack and Mrs. Pendleton were discussing her garden when Gus returned home with several bags of groceries. He and Mack hit if off right away. "Gus, you probably know Judy, the ER nurse; she told me you saw what happened."

"Yeah, I saw it. I was standing outside under the drive-up portico and just looking around the parking lot. It was just a few minutes before midnight, and I was about to go back in to punch the time clock when I heard loud voices comin' from the parking lot. You could tell right off it was an argument, but I didn't get the gist of everything they said. It didn't last long. But I'm sure I heard the nurse yell, 'No, Harry, don't!' Yep, that's what she said before he hit her."

Mack rolled his head back and muttered, "That bastard! It was her ex-husband. I had a run-in with him a few months back."

Gus said, "I called 911 right away, but the guy was long gone when the cops got here. If you know who it was, the Morris Plains PD opened an investigation and will want to talk to you. They couldn't interview the poor girl yet, so all I could give them was the guy's name was probably Harry."

"I'll go there next, Gus. Thanks for the help."

Back in the car and on the phone, Mack said, "Nezzie, look up a guy named Harry or Harold Lund. Should be in his mid-forties, a little under six feet, with brown hair. Might have a criminal record, too. Get back to me ASAP, please."

When Mack pulled into the Morris Plains PD parking lot, his phone buzzed. Nezzie reported, "This dude does have a criminal record, Mack. State Police website has him goin' back into the late nineties. Mostly petty stuff, but there are several assault and battery charges. One looks like it's a domestic case."

"Thanks, Nezzie. Gotta go."

The Morris Plains detective was grateful for the heads-up on Harry Lund. Mack described his own run-in with Harry and that the guy was likely obsessed with Penny. The detective told Mack they would make it a priority and scoop him up by the end of the day.

"That's great. Would you let me know when you have something?"

"No sweat."

Mack returned to the hospital only to learn that Penny was still unconscious. Bob had joined Brenda, and both were waiting for him. Bob took Mack by the arm and started walking him down the hall. "I was able to talk to one of the doctors. He said that Penny might have a hairline skull fracture, but the X-ray doesn't provide a clear enough view. When she wakes up, they want to do an MRI, to clear that up. The good news is her brain isn't swelling and the EEG keeps coming back normal."

"She must've been hit pretty hard."

"I've been poking around a little. One of the other nurses said whatever hit her broke the skin open, as well as the other damage. Mack, they seem to think it could've been something like a metal bar or a tire iron." Higgins stopped and turned Mack around. "Who the hell would do such a thing?"

"It was her ex-husband, Harry Lund. If I ever get my hands on him…"

"I know, I know. In the meantime, we need to be here to support Penny. That can come later, right?"

CHAPTER
Thirty-Seven

Once I make up my mind, I am full of indecision.
Oscar Levant – American musician,
author, actor, comedian

Day two of jury deliberations

*T*he jury foreman folded the note for the judge. It was the
third such message sent from the jury room in the past two
days. He handed it out to the bailiff posted outside the jury room.

Avery Reddy and Boyd Richards stayed within reach of
the court, sometimes hanging out in the small conference room
down the hall or at the coffee shop on the main floor of the courthouse. The tension was building.

"Why is it taking so long, Avery? They've been at it for two days. Isn't this a little unusual? What does it mean?" Boyd was becoming unglued.

"There's no telling what it means for sure, but most would say there is a heated discussion goin' on in that jury room. It would seem we got through to somebody, Boyd. The question now is whether or not they are able to hold out. Remember, it has to be one hundred percent, either way. I think it looks good for us!"

Avery's cell phone rang, "Mr. Reddy, this is Bonnie, Judge Frankel's law clerk calling. The judge needs you and Ms. Cummings in his chambers. Can you be here in ten minutes?"

"We'll be there."

Meanwhile, Sheila Cummings had been cloistered in her office and was relieved when the law clerk called her. *I wonder why Frankel isn't calling us back into the courtroom. Why his office?*

Judge Frankel, his robe off and in shirtsleeves, was staring out his office window when Sheila and Avery arrived, both at the same time. He turned to them with a sour look. "Well, folks, it looks like the jury is at an impasse. I sent them back three times to reconsider; but each time they came back deadlocked. I have no choice but to declare a hung jury. The prosecutor will have leave to reopen, and bail will be continued." He shook his head. "I can't blame either of you for this, and I think my actions were impartial, as well." He frowned at Sheila. "It may be that the murder-one charge scared some of them. That might've been overreach, Ms. Cummings, who knows? Okay, let's call the jury back in and put this mess on the record."

Avery met up with an anxious Boyd Richards in the hallway and gave him the news. Boyd blew up. He flailed his arms around and cried, "Oh my God. We have to go through this all over again? Avery, I just don't think I can handle it!"

"Maybe, maybe not. It depends on the prosecutor. But with Sheila in charge of the case, you can bet she will want to." Avery put his hand on Boyd's shoulder and said, "Next time, she will be better prepared and will anticipate our moves. We will have the same benefit; but, frankly, Boyd, it works more for the prosecutor than the defense. Just hang in there. We'll get through this together."

Boyd moaned. "In the meantime, my reputation is shot. I can't even get involved with my clients. Their boardrooms are buzzing over this. I am being shunned at the club. It's ruining me one way or the other." He walked with his head down and his shoulders slumped— a near broken man.

As they descended the stairs and headed out toward the parking lot, Avery said, "Boyd, maybe Mack and Higgins are right. Now that we have some more time, we should think about approaching it differently." He stopped walking and turned to Boyd, his attitude upbeat. "Maybe *we* can catch the bastard who killed Callie. The assistant prosecutor and some of the cops think you did it; so, they aren't gonna work it as an open case, but we can. According to Mack, Chief Worten is sympathetic. So, what do you think?" This new revelation ran contrary to everything he believed and practiced as a criminal lawyer; yet he could not deny that something different was called for in this case.

Boyd replied, "Avery, I've had enough. My family has been shattered by all this. I've lost my Callie..." His head down, he started to sob. After a deep breath, he looked back up at the court-house, tears streaking his face, and said, "They put me through this and now it starts again? Tell you what, Avery, we *do* need to take the initiative. I'm done with being a victim. Let's give Mack and Higgins all the support they need. This has to stop! We need to go on offense."

At that same moment, Sheila Cummings left the court dejected. She didn't lose; but she didn't win, either. She felt that a hung jury was a win of sorts for the defense, yet it left everyone hanging: ergo, the term *hung jury*. She'd no sooner arrived back at her office when a call came in from Congressman Barrett. "What happened, Sheila? I thought your evidence was solid: witnesses as to the infidelities, forensic evidence, what more did you need?"

"Wow, you heard about this fast. Nothing like having ears in the courthouse, huh, Congressman? So, you practiced law at one time, sir. You know how unpredictable juries can be. Remember the O.J. trial?"

"Please, Sheila, spare me. Apples and oranges. Simpson was a famous black athlete, actor, and all-around celebrity. That jury was looking for any reason to dump the case. Besides, the cops screwed the evidence up. Here we have an arrogant lawyer who thinks he's above it all and you have all the evidence you would ever need in your favor. You *are* going to give it another go, right?"

"I cannot imagine letting this lie." Her confidence returned, she said, "Of course, we will refile. It will take a month or so to review everything and file new charges. Judge Frankel hinted that I should stick with murder- two. He thinks that would be more appropriate and not overkill. What do you think?"

"Whatever. Just get a conviction this time!" Barrett hung up abruptly.

Disgusted, Sheila just shook her head.

CHAPTER
Thirty-Eight

If you must eat crow, eat it while it's young and tender.

Thomas Jefferson – Former American president and a founding father

Two days after the hung jury

Avery Reddy and Boyd Richards waited in Avery's office for the arrival of Mack and Higgins. "You know, Boyd, as a defense attorney, this might be antithesis to every nerve in my body, but it does give rise to a certain panache. I mean going after the killer, *ourselves*."

"Let's not get ahead of ourselves, Avery. We should give Mack and Higgins all the latitude, encouragement, and expenses they need. If anyone can dig this out, that pair can. At the same time, let's keep out of their way, okay? We're lawyers, not investigators."

"Yeah, I hear you. They should be here any time now."

When Mack and Higgins entered the fancy conference room, Higgins started right in. "I hear somebody hung a jury. Too bad they didn't include the lawyers!" Mack went into his act: he started looking around at all the shelves of books and said, "You know, Avery…"

"Okay, Mack, cut the 'craperoni!' No, I don't use all the books, okay?"

Mack and Higgins chuckled as they took their seats. Mack said, "Sorry we are a little late; we made a stop at the hospital to see Penny."

"How's the poor girl doing?" Avery said, genuinely concerned.

"Much better. She's allowed to get up and walk a little more each day. She gets dizzy spells, but the doctor says it's to be expected. I think she will be just fine, and thanks for asking."

"Did they catch the guy?"

"Oh yeah!" Bob Higgins wasn't going to let the best part of that story go without details. "You see, when they put the jerk into a holding cell, they allowed us into the jail to visit him, through the bars, of course. The Morris Plains cops are charging him with attempted murder and atrocious assault and battery. I mean, they had him dead to rights. They even found the tire iron in his trunk with some of Penny's blood and hair stuck to it. What an idiot! But here's the best part: Mack made him a deal. He told him, 'Harry, if you plead out, I won't make a special request of the prison to put you in with the biggest love-deprived Bubba they can find. If you plead not guilty and are convicted, which will surely happen, you get to meet Bubba, up close and personal. Now, if by some remote chance you should go free, you have me to deal with. Remember?' Then Mack reached into the cell and grabbed Lund by the nose and squeezed." Bob was really enjoying telling the story.

"All I did was tweak his nose a little," Mack said.

Bob would have none of that. "Some tweak! It brought tears to his eyes. We learned later the dude jumped at a plea. He told his court-appointed mouthpiece to shut up and do the paperwork. We laughed our asses off."

Mack said, "On a serious note, it's much better this way. He won't be bothering Penny anymore. He's already done enough. Almost killed her, the bastard."

"Well," said Avery, "I hope it works out for you two." Avery shifted uncomfortably in his chair, giving off that, "I have some-thing to say, but don't know how to start" look.

Mack helped him out. "Ahem... Avery, I understand you want to talk to Bob and me about doing some follow-up work on your case. Is that right?" He openly winked at Higgins.

"Okay. You were right, Mack. I'll eat crow, but just in this case." Avery wasn't going to concede his deep beliefs regarding criminal defense and his role in it. "Catching this guy is gonna be the only way I can see to get Boyd back as much of his former life as possible. It's not enough to get him off. He needs to be completely vindicated in the public's eye, as well. Any ideas?"

"I've been thinking about this. When Harlan Getz, the insurance guy, was killed by the same man who killed your wife, Boyd, he fell off his money train. I'm pretty sure he's back at conning insurance company claims staffs, just like before. The challenge is uprooting the current set of phony claims. We need to come up with something on that level to flush him out."

"Thought about how to do that?" Boyd slid forward in his chair. He was anxious to hear a solid plan.

"Yeah, I think so. I have some contacts in the New Jersey Insurance Fraud Division in Trenton—all retired cops. If we can get them onboard, we can reach out to every insurance claims staff in the state. All I have to do is go down there with one of the adjusters from Getz's office and show them the phony files we've unearthed thus far. That should whet their appetite, and when I throw in three murders, we should see them shift into high gear."

Boyd and Avery were nodding their heads when Boyd said, "See, Avery? Let's leave these guys alone. Let them do what they want." He turned to Mack and went on, "Good idea, Mack. Go for it. Cost is no object."

The group then fell to discussing all three murders. They all agreed that the killer murdered Callie and the tennis pro to cover up the Getz killing, as well as the insurance scam.

They all shook their heads in contempt when Higgins sarcastically commented, "He was just tying up loose ends."

CHAPTER
Thirty-Nine

If you want to make God laugh, tell him your plans.
Woody Allen – American actor, author, comedian

Mack and Higgins headed for the parking lot after the meeting. Higgins said, "I'm sure you've considered that a blanket notification from the fraud division could alert the perp, and we'll never hear from him again."

"I know. That's why it has to be handled carefully with only the right people knowing about it. The fraud division has its own contacts in the industry. They know the territory. And I'm glad Avery is onboard with us now. We have a free hand, Bob. Let's not screw it up!"

Mack returned to United Risks Mutual and met with claims manager Charles Howard. "Mr. Howard, we are going to get to the bottom of the Harlan Getz murder, but I need your help."

"I checked in with our home office, Mr. Mackey, and I was told to cooperate in any way possible with the investigation. How can we help?"

"I have an appointment with the insurance fraud division to go over what we know. I want to bring them into this. My belief is the killer is back at his scams with some other company or companies. That's the only way we're gonna catch this guy. I need someone from your office to go with me to Trenton to help lay out the case to the division. I think they would respond more positively if an insurance company is directly involved. Can you help me?"

"Not only will I help you, I'll go with you, myself."

Several days later, Mack and Mr. Howard drove south from Somerville on Route 202 to Flemington, then south again on Route 31 to the state government building complex in Trenton. The New Jersey Insurance Fraud Division was located on a side street in an old converted Victorian-style building. Mack and

Howard met with George Rankin, a former North Plainfield detective Mack knew from his days on the Plainfield PD.

"Hey, Mack. Great to see ya! How's the P.I. biz going?" George was an amiable, tall, lanky man in his early fifties.

"Hello, George. Thanks for taking the time to see us." They shook hands and the receptionist buzzed them into the inner offices of the division. Seated in a small conference room, Mack filled George in on the problem. "George, we have a guy who was supporting himself by scamming an insurance claims department. Something went wrong and he murdered a claims man named Harlan Getz. Then he covered his tracks by killing two more people. I would bet everything he is back to phony insurance claims, because it's what he does."

Rankin turned to the claims manager. "Mr. Howard, I see you've brought something with you. Would this be some sort of documentation on this subject?"

"Yes, what I have, together with what Mack has developed, should be everything you will need to review this. I couldn't bring all the actual claims files with me, but I compiled a fact sheet with exhibit copies that leaves no doubt we were scammed. You can keep it; I have copies, as does Mack." His head bowed and with a touch of humiliation, Mr. Howard continued, "Unfortunately, our man Getz was involved in the scam, too. For that, we are upset and embarrassed. My superiors are putting together a manual for our claims staff to prevent this from happening in the future. We want to work with the division on this, Mr. Rankin."

George Rankin, empathizing with the claims manager's last comment, re-directed the conversation, "The old inside man/ outside man scam, huh, Mack?"

"Yup. Do you think the division will go along with us here?"

"First I have to sell it upstairs. I think my director will see the advantage of working with a claims manager with a fraud problem. That's a no-brainer. As far as the murders are concerned, I can already hear it: 'That's not what we do here, George.' Not to worry, Mack. I will put a proposal together we can all live with."

Mack warned, "Just one thing, George. If we do this wrong, the perp will catch on and disappear. Can you keep control of it? I mean, as far as whatever you put out to the companies?"

"I hear ya, Mack. I already have an idea on that score. Let's get this sonovabitch!"

Mack added, "Before he kills again!"

CHAPTER
Forty

They gave each other a smile with a future in it.

Ring Lardner – American sports columnist and satirist

*P*enny was seated in the side chair in her room doing a crossword puzzle when Mack peeked in. "Any time for me, Ms. Money Penny?"

Excited to see him, Penny said, "My dragon slayer has come back to me! Come in here, you nice man. Did you know you have all the nurses around here swooning?"

A quick kiss on the forehead, then a longer one where it belonged, earned them a quiet private moment. Now, forehead to forehead, neither wished the moment to pass.

"Mack, I... I don't want to say anything stupid or presumptuous, but..."

He put two fingers on her lips, "Stop. You don't have to. I feel the same way. Let's take it a step at a time, Penny. I haven't felt this way in a long time." He lifted his head and grinned, "And it feels good."

Satisfied for the moment, Penny shifted to serious. "What happened with Harry?"

"He's being charged with attempted murder and atrocious assault and battery. He'll be going away for a long time. You needn't worry about him anymore. Oh, and yes his nose hurts."

"You hit him?" She half-smiled and added, "Again?"

"I tweaked him." Mack explained his ultimatum to Harry. "I think I convinced him to plead guilty for a lesser sentence. If he does, you won't have to testify. Let's hope."

"I'm sorry you got dragged into this, Mack. Harry was the biggest mistake I've ever made." She turned a pensive gaze to the sunlight streaming through her hospital room window.

"I'm sorry you were hurt, but ya gotta look at it this way: Harry gets the credit for introducing us, right? He might not appreciate that." They both laughed. "You get yourself better and out of here, and we'll start enjoying the life we've both earned."

"Why, Mack, you almost sound positive," she teased.

"Been a long time comin' for that, too. *You* get the credit there."

Mack picked up Penny at the hospital three days later and drove her home. On the way, they left the highway and stopped at a Starbucks in Pluckemin. "Mack, you have no idea how good it feels to be out here and, I can't explain it, the feeling of freedom. As a nurse, you would think I would understand what it's like to be a patient." She shook her head. "I guess I'll be more empathetic to my patients from now on."

Mack laughed, "I can't imagine you not being considerate of your patients. You are the most lighthearted and insightful person I've ever met. All I know is I like being with you, Penny."

"Me too, Mack. It's too bad we didn't meet years ago. Wait, I didn't mean anything toward your marriage to Margaret; it's just that we do seem to get along well, don't we?

"Yes, we do, and I don't take any offense. I know what you meant."

"Some of my choices in the past have been, shall we say, lacking in common sense? Harry was the worst. God! He almost killed me!" She fingered the recently removed stitch marks within her hairline.

"Well, he didn't kill you. I'd like to think that Harry has changed both our lives for the better, Penny." He reached across the table and took her hand. "But let's not let Harry into our thoughts anymore, okay?"

"How is it, Mack, you always say the right thing?"

"Now, that's a first, believe me."

Penny hesitated a moment then said, "Mack, you seem a little preoccupied lately. I don't mean to pry. Anything wrong?

"I'm sorry, if it shows. Yeah, we are working on a serious case that has us a bit baffled,"

"Can you tell me about it?

Mack went over the entire case for Penny. She was intrigued and asked good questions. "It seems to me this guy got caught up in his own web," she said. "It's like a domino effect: once he got started, one thing led to another, deeper and deeper. Do you think he would kill again if he had to?"

"No doubt in my mind, Penny." Signaling they should be going, Mack paid the check. Penny was tired and wanted to relax in her own surroundings, so Mack kissed her goodnight at her doorstep and walked down the hall to his own place.

Mack called Charles Howard at the insurance company and put in the request for the copies of checks, then called Bob Higgins. "Hey, Bob. Know any good handwriting experts?"

"Yeah. There's guy in the state police... what's his name? It'll come to me. What's up?"

"I want to compare the perp's handwriting in the insurance claim file with the endorsements on checks we should be getting back from the company soon." Mack continued, "Bob, I also need their facial-recognition expert, if you can squeeze that in."

"I got it: his name is Garretson. Al Garretson does the hand-writing analysis. I can give him a call and see if we can get him in on this. I don't know the facial-recognition guy. But, come to think about it, you will probably do better if Chief Worten calls down there. I think he has more oomph than I do anymore."

"Thanks, Bob. Will do."

CHAPTER
Forty-One

The best-laid plans of mice and men often go awry.
Robert Burns – Scottish poet and lyricist

Six weeks after the trial

*G*ordon Krone, aka Bruce, was running low on cash. He went through the last of the bank accounts set up with Getz and considered going back into the insurance scam business but thought better of it. *They might be looking for me now that the case against that politician went down, so I'd better stay away from that. I'm not the liquor store holdup type. No, I'll stick to what works* for *me but without the insurance angle.*

Gordon checked out businesses he thought would fall for this new approach. Instead of looking for big insurance payoffs that took months to play out, he could still fake the slip and fall injury but look for an immediate cash settlement from the target. It worked—not always—but often enough to be worthwhile. "Gee whiz, I don't really want to make a big deal out of this, like an insurance claim or a lawsuit. Couldn't you just pay me for a doctor's visit and a little for my trouble? I'll probably need a prescription, too." More often than not, the store manager would pay him a couple hundred dollars to make him go away. Several, on the other hand, saw the scam for what it was and hustled him out of the store, threatening to have him locked up.

Unfazed by the occasional rejection, he persevered. He went for small businesses in low-income neighborhoods where few bothered to buy insurance. This new scam did little more than help him stay afloat. He longed for the days when the insurance checks kept coming. Even after the money split with Harlan Getz, he was pocketing decent money back then.

There was one hitch, however. In most cases, he had to leave a name and address, together with short statement that he had no intention of suing the store. Everything went smoothly until the unexpected occurred. Saul Epstein, the owner of this and six other stores spread out in the Linden, Rahway and Elizabeth area had a question for his store manager. "What's this $300 expense, Josh? Your expense ledger doesn't spell it out."

"Oh, some guy fell down in the produce section and hurt his knee. I thought it was easier to just pay him something to go away rather than report it." Store manager Josh continued, "Besides, it was better than having our insurance premium go up for such a small claim. He was willing, so I paid him off."

"Never do that again," warned Epstein. "Do you have any paperwork on him?"

"I have his name and address somewhere here," Josh said as he rummaged through his untidy desk. "Here it is, Warren Stewart, 126 Elizabeth Ave., Elizabeth, NJ, Apartment 204."

Epstein said, "Good. I'm putting this in to the insurance company for reimbursement." He figured, *We pay enough all year in premiums. Might as well get some use out of it.*

Mack checked in with George Rankin at the insurance fraud division on a regular basis. Six weeks had gone by with no reports to the division of a suspicious nature, but this morning was different. Rankin called Mack and was upbeat, "Mack, I have something for you. Epstein Corner Markets, an insured of Commonwealth Mutual Insurance Group, turned in a claim earlier this week, and the name and address for the claimant matches one on the list you gave us."

"Any chance you could give the insurance company a call, George? I want to follow up with them and the insured, Epstein, and it would help if they knew you approved."

"You got it, pal."

After picking up a copy of the claim at Commonwealth, Mack went to Epstein's corporate office in Elizabeth. Saul Epstein provided Mack with the original signed statement and release by "Warren Stewart" setting forth his "payment in full for injuries sustained."

Mack located 126 Elizabeth Avenue in Elizabeth and smiled. He walked into the UPS Store and looked around. On the left wall, he found what he was looking for. The section consisted of more than one hundred small mailboxes, some with and some without keys in the locks. There was #204, the "residence" of Warren Stewart.

"Come in, Mack. Good to see you. Please, have a seat." Prosecutor Raymond Lant's office was on the spartan side, considering his high office. "Bill Worten is on his way down. He'll be here in a minute. I understand you have a break in the Richards case?"

"Could be. We set it up with the insurance fraud division for insurance companies in the state to run submitted claims against the list of phony names and addresses we know the Getz killer used— by the way, also likely the killer of Callie Richards and Johnny Campbell." Mack paused and was pleased to see the prosecutor nod in agreement. He continued, "They did this with a computer program. In that way, there was no possible leaking of the project to an inside co-conspirator... Hey, Bill." Chief Worten entered the room and sat down next to Mack.

"Okay, I follow you. What can we do to help?" The prosecutor began making notes.

"I checked the address the claimant gave, and, no surprise, it is a mailbox in a UPS Store on Elizabeth Avenue. I didn't even try to get the clerk to allow me entry into the box, 'cause I knew that was not gonna happen. But she would have to cooperate if we get a search warrant for the box, as well as the paperwork backing it up. Anything you would be interested in?" Mack looked back and forth between them and added, "Fellas, this may be the break we've been looking for."

Both Raymond Lant and Chief Worten nodded their heads and grinned. Lant said, "Great work, Mack. Let's hope it pans out. I will get to work on the search warrant, but you need to sit down with Bill and give us all the details for the affidavit for probable cause. If you get it done soon, I think I know a friendly judge who will grant us the warrant."

Later that same day, Worten and Mack, along with two other detectives, descended on the UPS Store and executed the search warrant. The clerk cooperated fully, but she had never seen the owner of the box in the store. There was nothing in Box #204, but the backup paperwork was another matter. "Warren Stewart" gave another address as his residence, but it was the copy of the driver's license in the file that caused a stir. "This D.L. is as phony as they come," said Worten. He passed the copy around to the officers who, after studying it, all concurred.

Chief Worten said, "I have the fingerprint boys on the way. Maybe they can grab a print off the box door." But the way he said it wasn't exactly encouraging. "No telling who else touched it, you know. I bet that address he gave is another dead end."

One of the young detectives said, "You can bank on that!"

Mack whipped around, "What did you just say?"

Taken by surprise, the detective repeated, "I just said you can bank on that, sir."

Mack gave himself a "Coulda had a V-8" smack. "Of course! Bill, we goofed, big time. The insurance company wrote this guy checks. Checks, Bill. Deposits, endorsements, bank... get it?"

"Ah... You're right, Mack. Let's get that claims manager locating both-side copies of those checks. We'll identify the bank and maybe get to this guy that way. Good thinking."

Mack pocketed a copy of the phony driver's license. As they all left the UPS store, he let himself have a glimmer of hope. *Maybe we finally have a break in this case.*

Back at the office, he showed the phony license to Inez. She said, "Too bad this isn't bigger. We might be able to get a better look at him."

Mack brightened. "You're right, Nezzie. Call Phil at the print place and see if he can do anything with this, will ya? I got a date with a freckle-faced cutie."

"Give her my best, Mack."

"No, I'll give her *my* best."

CHAPTER
Forty-Two

It is through science that we prove, but through
intuition that we discover.

Henri Poincare – French mathematician and philosopher

Three days later a meeting was held in the Union County
Prosecutor's Office. Present were Chief Bill Worten,
Mack, Higgins, Charles Howard from United Risks Mutual,
and two New Jersey State Troopers from the Identification and
Forensics Bureau: Detective Albert Garretson and Detective
Sergeant Robert Jennings.

Detective Garretson signed for the original claims releases
and copies of the checks received from the insurance company.
He promised to have his handwriting analysis back within a
week. Claims manager Howard advised there were five banks
involved in the insurance scam. He pointed out that transfers

occurred between those banks, as well. He gave Mack a list of the banks and a second copy of the checks issued to the phony claimant under a dozen different names.

Sergeant Jennings, the facial-recognition expert, began discussing a technology new to law enforcement involving a computerized program that evaluated photographs, videotapes, and disks, as well as artist renderings of individuals. "It takes the data in and evaluates all the potential variabilities, including unmasking attempts at disguise. We have taken the standard facial-recognition program used by the TSA and other security groups and enhanced it to spot biometric aberrations—that is, anomalies that don't comport with the remainder of the subject's normal appearance. It takes into account bone structure, age, and weight gain and loss, as well as other factors."

Chief Worten piped up, "Can you put that into English, Sergeant?"

Jennings smiled and answered, "What it means is when a person tries to change his appearance, from one image to another, the computer recognizes it and has the ability to erase the change and put forth what the person should look like without the disguise. It works pretty well, actually."

Mack asked, "What if we had a number of separate photos, videos and artist renderings of what we believe to be the same person. Can the program discern all the variants and come up with what the undisguised person should look like?"

"Yes, and because you have many samples from different sources, the program would be even more capable of evaluating the data. It has been very helpful, so far. Unfortunately, as a new technology, the courts have not accepted it as expert evidence, but we are hopeful it will be soon. As you know, science lags along behind the law when it comes to admissibility in court."

Chief Worten added, "But we can still use it as an investigative tool, right?"

Jennings was accommodating. "True, and we would be happy to put it to work for you."

Mack said to Chief Worten, "Bill, ask the prosecutor to work up a subpoena for the banks, because we know they're not gonna give voluntarily. Oh, you might also throw in a request to review all bank security tapes that relate to the day the checks were cashed or deposited."

"Tall order, Mack, but I think I can convince Raymond to work with us on this. He's been on board, so far."

As Mack and Higgins left the meeting, Mack commented, "My intuition tells me we are on the right track this time, Bob."

"The only real valuable thing is intuition," answered Bob in a haughty way.

Mack gibed, "Where did that come from?"

Affecting a snooty demeanor, Higgins said, "Not one for being pretentious, I happen to know it was Albert Einstein."

"Oh, of course." They left Elizabeth and fought traffic back to Mack's office.

"Nezzie, anything from Phil on the enlargement?"

Nezzie needed a little love and her sing-song sarcasm showed it: "Hello, Nezzie. Having a good day, Nezzie? Working hard in this one-woman office, Nezzie? Everything okay, Nezzie? Have lunch today, Nezzie? No, all I get is 'Anything from Phil on the enlargement?' Not even a 'Hello.'" She glared at Mack.

Higgins, never at a loss for words, said, "Maybe I should wait in the car until the shootin' stops?"

Mack was contrite. "Sorry, Nezzie. We've been going nuts over this case. Everything you do in here saves me time out there. You are the linchpin. You *are* appreciated and you know it."

Nezzie wiggled in her seat, eyes batting and attitude softening, "Really, Mack?"

"Of course. So?"

"On your desk, ya big lug," her smug expression revealing it was all an act.

The enlargement of the phony driver's license photo was on an 8 x 10-inch rigid mounting board. The focus was acceptable, and the color was vivid. Mack nodded his head. "Yeah, I think this is the type of thing Sergeant Jennings can make use of. Can you run this down to him, Bob? We're going to start collecting photos on this guy, as soon as I can get around to the banks Mr. Howard was talking about."

"Sure thing, Mack." Higgins left for NJSP headquarters in West Trenton.

CHAPTER
Forty-Three

Everything comes to him who hustles while he waits.
Thomas Edison – American inventor and businessman

ack took the list of banks and subpoenas for each one and hit the road. His first stop was The First Unity Hudson Bank on Paterson Plank Road in Secaucus. He drove north on the New Jersey Turnpike to Exit 17, then to the narrow, congested streets of Secaucus, composed of mixed residential and business neighborhoods. Mack recalled his seventh-grade history teacher's lesson: *The Paterson Plank Road spans the three counties of Passaic, Bergen and Hudson and was originally lain in Colonial times. The road connected the City of Paterson with the Hudson River waterfront, just across from the island of Manhattan. Originally, plank roads consisted of laying boards side-to-side to prevent coach and wagon wheels from getting* *bogged down in soft or swampy ground.* Mack thought, *Funny how some thoughts just appear out of nowhere. Like, "...you can bank on that."*

At the bank, he met with the manager, Roger Fedoric. Once Fedoric understood the issues at stake, he was fully cooperative but said he needed to fax a copy of the subpoena to the bank's attorney before providing any information about a depositor. It took only half an hour for the law firm to call back after confirming the subpoena with the Union County Prosecutor's Office.

Fedoric looked up each of the phony names from Mack's list and found three with low balance accounts in the bank—one in each of three branches located in Secaucus, North Bergen and Jersey City. He was able to retrieve computerized copies of the driver's licenses presented for identification at the time the accounts were opened. Once they appeared on Fedoric's computer screen, both he and Mack were startled to see the resemblance between all three. "Looks like the same guy," Fedoric said, pointing to the screen. He went on, "This one has a thin moustache and dark-rimmed glasses, and this one's cheeks are fatter. Look at the way the hair is slicked back on this one."

Mack said, "Obviously, the same guy. Not really sophisticated disguises but enough to have it work for him. I will need printouts on all of this, Roger. How long before you can send me copies of the security tapes showing him setting up these accounts?"

"That will take a little longer. I have to go to the security company where the disks are stored, but we'll make this a priority. We, in the banking industry, do not appreciate this fraudulent identity stuff. Here, take one of my cards and check in with me early next week."

All five banks that Mack visited accommodated his every request. He came back to the prosecutor's office with copies of identification photographs from twelve branches of the five banks involved.

"Damn, this guy looks familiar, Mack." Chief Worten held up two of the photos to the light, comparing one to the other.

Mack agreed, "I thought so, too. I guess what makes it confusing is there are so many, and the subtle variations play with your mind."

"Once we get the video of him setting up the accounts, we should get this all down to Sergeant Jennings at the NJSP lab and see if he can do anything with it."

"My thoughts, exactly, Bill."

CHAPTER
Forty-Four

The life of the law has not been logic,
it has been experience.
Oliver Wendell Holmes, Jr. – Former Associate
Justice of U.S. Supreme Court

Sheila Cummings refiled the criminal case against Boyd Richards. This time, the complaint would be murder in the second degree, more suitable under the circumstances—more so, since Judge Frankel's comment after the hung jury. "Chief Worten, I want you personally to serve this complaint on the defendant, and do it as soon as possible, understand?"

"Right. Do we have any new evidence?" His question was more of a sarcastic remark.

Sheila looked sideways at Worten. "We don't need any, Chief. We had him dead to rights the first time. It was that jury—and

Avery Reddy's sickening pandering to them. I won't let him get away with it this time."

Worten smiled as he turned away. "I was just wondering."

Gordon Krone received his subpoena to appear as a witness again. *I wonder if that bitch has her act together this time. I should give her a call and see what's going on.* He returned to his pushups, *103... 104... 105...*

Avery Reddy called Boyd Richards and set up a meeting to discuss strategy. He also called Mack and asked him and Higgins to join in that meeting.

Mack and Higgins showed up with a cardboard box full of photographs, video disks and the artist renderings made from descriptions supplied by Maria Sanchez and Alex DeFazio at the insurance company. Mack presented the information methodically, placing each photograph on the conference table, while

Higgins handled the computer showing the security images from the bank. "We haven't received anything back from the state police guys yet," Mack reported. "That is, the handwriting expert and the facial-recognition sergeant. When we do I will get it right to you, Avery." While the group pored over the photos, Mack went on, "Boyd? Avery? As you know, we have been busy since the hung jury. I believe in my bones we are getting close to the truth here. I wish I had an answer for you today, but I don't. All I can say is it is coming along well. I want to take a few minutes to go over the timeline that my secretary put together. Any objections?"

Boyd Richards replied, "Will this help my case, Mack?"

"I believe it will. We know you didn't kill Callie, Boyd. There are two other murders that are connected, and putting all the facts together makes a convincing case for your innocence."

"Let's have it."

Mack propped up Nezzie's chart showing dates, times, people, places and how they related to one another. More than a flow chart, it was a detailed accounting, from hour to hour, with overlapping instances and how they combined to simplify Mack's assertions.

"According to the medical examiner, the insurance claims man, Harlan Getz, first fell down the stairs. Some of his injuries were such that the M.E. believes he was alive during the fall. Afterwards, however, someone finished Getz off by brutally breaking his neck in many places. That degree of injury could not have occurred with just the fall alone. We know Getz was alive and well at 5:00 p.m. when the claims staff left at the end of their workday. Now, let's jump over to Callie's timeline. We know from Johnny Campbell that Callie left his loft a little after 5:00 p.m., the same time period Getz met his demise and less than one hundred feet away." Mack turned the chart around to show Nezzie's blowup of Google Earth's aerial view. "So, there's the alley where Callie had to walk through to get to her car. There is a side door from the insurance company's office into that alley, right about... here. It's not exactly guesswork to believe Callie and the perp somehow interacted in that alley."

Avery asked, "How do we know he used that door?"

"Knowing he just committed murder, don't you think he would want to leave quickly and avoid the front door? Besides, up to now, this guy was probably just a fraudster bilking insurance companies out of money. I think he would head for the nearest exit, and that's where that door was." Avery began nodding his head in agreement midway through Mack's explanation.

Mack resumed, "Think about it. This guy knows Callie can identify him, so he follows her home. He comes back the next day and kills her. I spoke with Chief Worten about the house for sale to the rear of the Richards property. He now agrees it's possible for the perp to have parked his car in that driveway and hidden in those bushes in back waiting for Callie to come out."

"Bastard!" Boyd's eyes were filling up.

"I know, Boyd. Sorry, but we have to get this out"

"Go on."

"When Bob and I interviewed Johnny Campbell, I think the perp was watching the front of the insurance company, so when the three of us walked down the alley together, he saw us. He assumed, and rightfully so, that Johnny was explaining Callie's route back to her car. But he didn't know enough from just watching us. He might've thought Johnny knew something about Callie's running into him in the alley. He had to do something about Johnny, and he did."

Mack sat down, and all were silent for a long moment. Bob Higgins spoke, "The problem with this theory—and I agree with it a hundred percent—is it is just that, a theory. We can't prove it yet. But it makes the most sense."

Avery said, "Let me put my two cents in here. If I were defending this perp, I would ask, 'Where's the beef?' It's all speculation. There are no witnesses, no forensics, no documentation, which means no case. And I think you all know it."

Mack answered, "Ah, but we are on the way to proving it, Avery. Once we identify the insurance fraudster, we'll have the Getz killer. Chief Worten and his crew can take it from there. Linking him to Callie and Johnny Campbell is just a matter of time and good police work. The problem we have been having is the guy's smart and has used multiple names and addresses.

He's even disguised himself enough to avoid easy recognition. I think he must be a cold-hearted psychopath to have killed so casually to avoid arrest on fraud charges. It started with Getz. Callie and Johnny Campbell were collateral damage. Loose ends, if you will."

Higgins again, "My alma mater, the NJSP, is finishing up with getting a good identifying photo of the perp. Once we have that, as Mack said, we will be on the road to proving you didn't kill your wife, Boyd. And that's what all this is about. Trust us a little longer, please."

CHAPTER
Forty-Five

*There is a thin line between genius and insanity. I have
erased this line.*

**Oscar Levant – American musician, author,
actor, comedian**

"**A**very, **Mack here. Just checking in with you.** I will be with the state police, Higgins and Chief Worten in the morning. Sounds like we are making progress. Please let Boyd know." He hung up from Avery's voicemail and flicked on the television, scanning for baseball scores.

The next morning the group met in the conference room at Chief Worten's office. The state troopers wasted no time. "Here's the evidence you need to show the handwriting is all the work of one person. It also matches the signature cards on the back accounts. It's all the same guy."

The facial-recognition expert laid out all the photos on the long table, making a comment about each one. "This is the enlargement of the fake driver's license you dropped off, Bob. Here is the still shot of the best of the bank security tapes. Some were not of the quality we needed, but this one was great. Here is the artist rendering from the two witnesses in the insurance company. From all this data, the computer considered all the variables and came up with a composite of what we believe your perp really looks like. Here it is."

Mack, Higgins and Worten leaned in closer. Worten was first to speak, "I know that face."

Mack said, "Me, too. Jeez. It looks just like that witness, what was his name? Oh yeah, Krone." Mack and Higgins looked up and stared at each other. Mack was first to speak, "Holy shit! You don't suppose..."

Higgins slowly nodded his head, "It's starting to make sense now. Of course, he's the perp, but he wants to be sure someone else is convicted, so he testifies against Boyd."

Mack jumped in. "He has the murder weapon, so all he has to do is plant the blood evidence in the 7-Eleven and lead the cops to it." He shook his head. "What a devious creep."

Worten reflected, "Actually, it's bold and genius. And he almost got away with it,"

"Almost? It depends what we do with what we have here," Mack said. "This is not enough for a murder complaint, let alone a conviction. We need more evidence on this guy." Mack was fired up. "Wait a second. If I remember right, wasn't he a corrections officer somewhere? He must have had a background done, and fingerprints and identification photo, right?"

Worten answered, "Yes! I'll get right on it."

"I'll find out where he lives and get as much as possible at that end. Guys? We have a direction to go in and a viable suspect." Mack was energized.

The state troopers added that they would be available to compare any known handwritings of Gordon Krone to the other evidence, as well as any subsequent photographic evidence that might come up.

CHAPTER
Forty-Six

In the field of observation, chance favors the prepared mind.
Louis Pasteur – French biologist, invented pasteurization

The same day, 3:15 p.m.

Mack met with Avery and Boyd and showed them the reports from the NJSP troopers, along with the computerized composite rendering of the person looking much like Gordon Krone. Avery was ecstatic. "You did it! I cannot believe this guy. What a pair of cajones!" He poured over the reports and photographs a second time. Deflation set in. "It's not enough. You have him on the insurance fraud, but nothing else. We know it's him but can't prove it yet."

Mack answered, "We know. Right now, we are all in the field pushing as hard as possible to come up with more, Avery. I'm goin' down to his trailer park and interview the manager. Bill Worten is pulling everything he can on Krone's past employment, along with his background check. Bob Higgins will be tailing him to see what else he's up to. Hang in there, Avery. We won't let you down."

The next morning, Bob Higgins took Interstate 78 directly to Union Township, New Jersey. After cruising around the area and spotting Krone's trailer, he parked in the side yard of a small manufacturing company a half-mile away on Springfield Avenue. Bob walked into the front office of the business and up to the reception window where a middle-aged woman was seated at a computer. "Hi there. Can I speak to the boss for a minute?"

"That would be Mr. Boise. He's out in the plant. Can I tell him what this is about?"

"Actually, I am a private investigator and it is a confidential matter." Bob knew that would generate a lot of interest without revealing his true purpose.

Shortly thereafter, Bob met with plant manager George Boise in his private office. "So, why on earth do I have the pleasure of meeting with a private investigator? Is my wife having me followed?" Mr. Boise, a fifty-something, heavy-set, cigar-smoking guy with a good-natured personality, pointed to a seat for Bob, as he dropped down into a leather chair behind his desk and studied Bob's business card.

"Well, if that were the case, Mr. Boise, I wouldn't be talking to you, would I?" Bob was used to being teased about his profession. "The reason I am talking to you is your parking lot. Let me explain. But first, do you have employees here?" He was setting Boise up mentally for what he was after.

"Of course, we have between forty-five and sixty on board, depending on our needs at the moment. Why do you ask?" Boise was becoming a little defensive, but his curiosity was piqued.

"Okay, then, I'm pretty sure you carry worker's compensation insurance, right?"

"Of course, what *is* your point, Mr. Higgins?"

"As a boss, yourself, you can appreciate insurance premiums and that some people inflate their claims, right? Well, I am working for an insurance company on such a case—no connection to you or your business here—and I need to be able to park in your parking lot to be able to follow the guy pushing the claim." Bob was stretching the facts a little, but he needed a perch.

"I see where you're going. You want to use my lot to watch someone."

"Yes, but it's only to wait for him to drive by. He's not located anywhere near you; just likely to drive by here. Do you mind?"

Higgins went into his Boy Scout act. "I thought it best to be straight up front and talk to you, rather than trying to sneak into your lot without permission. Wadda ya say?"

"As long as we don't get involved in any lawsuit, I don't see why not. Do you know how long you will be?"

"I would guess not more than a week or so—on and off—depending on how often he is back in this area. I do appreciate it."

"Okay. I'll go for it—again, as long as we won't be involved."

"You got it. Thanks."

Investigator Higgins, his surveillance point established safely, settled down to watching traffic flow up and down Springfield Avenue. He pulled out his file and reviewed the data he needed to accomplish his work: the plate number and description of the maroon 2012 Ford Explorer registered to Gordon Krone and his driver's license photograph. He set up his van by putting away anything loose or in the way, so he could move quickly when required. He waited, his video camera in his lap.

CHAPTER
Forty-Seven

The harder you work, the luckier you get.
Gary Player – Champion golfer, South Africa

*M*ack was in the Union area, too, though not in touch with Higgins. He parked in a space in front of a trailer with an "Office" sign posted in the window. He knocked and a woman's voice shouted, "Yeah, come on in."

The confining interior of the trailer was set up with a chest-high counter-top a couple of feet in front of Mack as he crossed the threshold. He didn't see anyone at first, then a woman Mack thought to be in her sixties popped up behind the counter with a black cat clutched to her belly. The woman was as disheveled as the trailer. Her worn print dress and washed-out green sweater had seen better days. A half-smoked cigarette dangling from her lips, she ranted, "Damned cat! Forever making me search for her. Probably looking for a spot to have another litter." She brazenly looked Mack up and down. "What do you want?" Then in a more calculating, yet genial way, "You're too well dressed to be looking for a trailer rental and too good lookin' to be lookin' for me." Though her smile exposed several missing teeth, it was nonetheless genuine.

Mack smiled back, "My name's Mack." He held out his hand. She shook it like a dockworker. "Mine's Wilma, but they call me 'Willie.'"

"Willie, can you keep a secret?"

"Secrets? Hell, you don't live in a trailer park and not have secrets, Mack. You a cop? You have that look."

"You have a good eye, Willie; but no, I'm not a cop." Mack handed her his business card. Willie put the glasses hanging on a cord around her neck up to her eyes, knocking a glowing ash off the cigarette. The cat escaped the falling ember and jumped down. "You're a P.I. Well, I wasn't far off, was I? What's up? Which of my local beauties is of interest to you?"

"Again, Willie, can you keep a secret?"

"Oh yeah. Just talk to Captain Hawkins here in Union. I keep him— shall we say—up-to- date with certain hopheads in the area. Know what I mean?"

Mack said, "It's about Gordon Krone, Know him?"

Her expression turned somber, and she said, "Something really weird about that guy. He comes and goes in different cars and vans. He's antisocial. Never talks with anybody. I swear, sometimes he looks different than he did the day before. I think he's a nut case. He never talks to me. He pays his trailer space rent with cash in an envelope through the slot." She pointed to the trailer door. "If you turn around and look straight out the window, that's his trailer, the one with the green and white metal awning over the door."

Mack peered through the window, "You can see him come and go from here?"

Willie smiled conspiratorially. "Could it be you might want me to help you keep tabs on him? What's he done?"

In a solemn manner, Mack drew closer and said, "Willie, this is serious business. I do not want him to know about this, understand? I can't be completely open with you right now, but he is in big trouble. If he catches you being curious, he might hurt you."

Willie reached under the counter and pulled out a snub-nosed .38 caliber Colt revolver. "This was my dearly departed's off-duty sidearm when he worked for the Elizabeth PD back in the seventies. Don't worry about Willie. My Eugene taught me well."

The gun was loaded. Mack could see the ends of the ammo rounds in the cylinders. "Okay, Willie, but don't take any chances with him."

Willie also mentioned that Krone often had different rental vans parked at his trailer. She said they were likely Enterprise rentals, because she's found rental receipt copies in his garbage.

"You mean you have access to his garbage?"

"Yep. That's the deal here. It's easier for me to pick up everybody's garbage than chasing it blowin' around the area when they don't bother to empty the bins themselves. These people ain't exactly what you would call environmentally responsible, Mack."

Mack was encouraged, "Would you keep any papers you find in his trash for me?"

"You bet. My pleasure." She put the pistol back in its place and gave Mack a warm smile. "You remind me of Eugene. Very serious and a gentleman."

There were no vehicles parked at Krone's trailer during Mack's visit. He was tempted to take a closer look at the trailer, but he didn't want to take a chance on Krone's return. Instead, he thanked Willie and promised to put in a good word with Captain Hawkins for her help. She, in turn, promised to call Mack and keep him current about Krone's comings and goings. Mack called Nezzie and told her to expect Willie's calls. Mack also called Bob Higgins.

"Bob, just got done at the trailer park. Krone is known to the manager, and she will keep us up on his activity. You should also know he rents vans from Enterprise, so you will be looking for more than just his Explorer."

"No problem. When I leave here, I will scope out the nearest Enterprise office. Early tomorrow morning I will come back and take down all their plates for future reference. Hey, I gotta a good perch here along Springfield, just a couple of blocks from the trailer park. I can't see him going in the other direction, so…"

Mack cut him short. "Sounds good, Bob. Gotta go and meet with Avery. He needs his hand held. The new trial isn't far away now."

CHAPTER
Forty-Eight

*Take time to deliberate; but when the time for action arrives,
stop thinking and go in.*

**Andrew Jackson – Soldier, statesman, and seventh
U.S. president**

Later that day

*A*ttorney Avery Reddy was unconsciously wringing
his hands as he greeted Mack in the Westfield law
office, a deep frown on his face. Avery's nervous behavior carried
into the conference room where Boyd Richards was reviewing
the latest set of transcripts from the first trial. Boyd didn't even
look up when they entered. It was apparent to Mack that he had
walked in during an uncomfortable situation.

Mack took a seat and ventured, "Pretrial jitters?"

No response from either. Half an awkward moment passed in silence.

"Okay. Am I here to offer advice and assistance or to referee a pissing match between two juvenile wannabe lawyers?"

Boyd was first. "We are in trouble here, Mack. We don't need smart-ass remarks from you." He looked back down at the paperwork. Avery's expression showed concurrence.

"No, you don't. What you do need is to pull together and stop your childish moping. We are making progress in the field. You know what the field is, don't you?" Mack looked back and forth between the two. "The field—that is where the real world is and where we come up with the fodder for your legal minds to chew on." Mack remained standing and pointed directly at the pair. "You guys can never seem to look beyond your files. You think everything hinges on those reams of paper in front of you. I don't entirely discount their value; but without facts, it's all bullshit!" Mack had had enough of the cerebral legal minds and intended to scold them back to reality.

Avery challenged Mack, "So, what great breakthrough have you uncovered today?"

"Higgins has Krone under surveillance. His trailer-park manager is being very helpful and—I have to say—at her own peril. Chief Worten called me a few minutes ago and reported that Krone was counseled by the prison psychiatrist before he quit. We also have a copy of Krone's entire personnel file. While you two are crying in your beer, we are swimming upstream, so let's get down to business and work this out, okay?"

Avery and Boyd exchanged sour looks, but grudgingly nodded their heads in agreement. As an afterthought, Avery said, "Shouldn't Bob be careful with this guy?"

"Don't worry about Higgins. He can handle himself. I'd be more worried about Krone, should it come to that."

Mack, having set the stage for some real dialogue, sat down and said, "So what's got your knickers in a twist today?"

"We have gone over the entire trial transcript and can't find anything we could or would do any better, Mack." Avery was frustrated. He continued, "In fact, Boyd's response to Sheila's questioning regarding his presumed behavior was the best anyone could offer. Don't forget, we surprised her when Boyd took the stand. But she has the advantage this time, because she knows our answers and has had the time to come up with a new approach. We, on the other hand, are left with the same old line as before. We are truly on defense—no pun intended."

"Avery? Boyd? As Bob Higgins would say, 'The fat lady ain't sang yet!' You guys need to lighten up. Now that we know who the perp is, it's only a matter of time before we trip him up. We have him under a microscope, and the good stuff is yet to come." Mack leaned closer to Avery across the conference table, "All we need is enough for Worten to apply for a search warrant for that trailer." Mack's head cocked, and he made a face that said, "Duh?"

Avery blinked a couple times. "You're right, Mack. We just don't think the way you do. It's a matter of action versus reaction. We need to act, and you guys are leading the charge." He looked over at Boyd for approval. He got it.

As Mack walked out, he threw over his shoulder, "You guys really need to get out into the sunlight. This paperwork is turning your brains to mush!"

CHAPTER
Forty-Nine

You always pass failure on your way to success.
Mickey Rooney – American actor and comedian

The next day, 8:45 a.m.

ob Higgins took down the license plates at Enterprise on Central Avenue in Union and then continued to his perch at the manufacturing company parking lot. He avoided passing through the trailer park as an unnecessary risk, as his surveillance of Krone would put his vehicle in the subject's presence enough. At midday, Gordon Krone drove past in his Explorer and Bob fell in behind, maneuvering so two other cars were between him and Krone, who drove directly to the Enterprise lot. It took only ten minutes for Krone to leave Enterprise in a new white Dodge minivan. Bob followed the

Dodge into the town of Carteret, and into the parking lot of a mini-mall on Roosevelt Avenue.

Krone left the van and entered a Dollar Store. Bob was able to back up his van close to the store's large window. He could see Krone walking around, pushing a shopping cart. Bob began videotaping. About ten minutes in, Krone found himself alone in one of the aisles. He took several small items from a shelf and scattered them over the floor. He then sat down on the floor and—from what Bob could see but not hear—began yelling and acting as if he were injured from a fall. Bob saw store employees rush to his aid, including a woman who seemed to be in charge.

Bob sat back in the van and replayed the videotape. He grinned and thought, *This is good stuff. Just what we need to show how this guy operates.*

Higgins grabbed his cell phone out of his pocket and called Mack. "You won't believe the video I just got of Krone, Mack. We never get the goods on someone actually committing the fraud, but I have it this time." He described the content of the videotape.

"Bob, what you have is gold! We do have a lot of evidence to present to a judge that there has been insurance fraud, but there's nothing like a videotape to drive home the point. Please get that over to Chief Worten, ASAP."

Mack had no sooner ended that call when his phone buzzed again. "Mack? This is Willie at the trailer park. I have something you might be interested in." Willie had retrieved papers from Krone's garbage bin. "I don't know what it means, but there's names and other stuff in his handwriting. You probably want to get these."

Mack drove to Union and met with Willie. She handed over previously crumpled pages of notebook paper. The writing was disciplined and uniform, just like that of other samples of Krone's handwriting. Along with grocery lists, Mack found references to small businesses and their addresses in seven nearby cities in Union and Essex counties. One of the businesses listed was the Dollar Store where Higgins videotaped Krone earlier that day. Willie also said that Krone had another Enterprise van in his driveway again.

Mack called Chief Worten. "Bill, let's pull the plug on this case. I think we have enough for a search warrant, but let's speak to the prosecutor for his take on it."

Early that evening, Chief Worten and Prosecutor Lant met to go over all the evidence. Lant dictated an affidavit for search warrant, which was signed by Worten. The prosecutor's secretary stayed late to type up the affidavit and the search warrant for the judge's signature. The most significant paragraph in the affidavit drew the connection between the Getz murder and the proximity to the Campbell loft down the alley that Callie Richards had to traverse to reach her car. It wasn't—in and of itself—enough for a murder conviction; but it didn't have to be.

It was enough for a search warrant. After all, there was irrefutable proof that the crime of insurance fraud had been committed and a strong inference that the murders followed. Prosecutor Lant and Chief Worten went before a county judge with their request for search warrant.

CHAPTER
Fifty

A fox should not be on the jury at a goose's trial.
Thomas Fuller – English churchman and historian

Monday, 9:10 a.m., - Second trial, Day One

oyd Richards entered the courtroom with his
attorney, Avery Reddy, and both took their places
at the defendant's table. As is the norm, a new judge presided
over this retrial. Judge Marvin Thomas was relatively new on
the bench, but was considered by members of the Union County
Bar Association to be a tough and fair jurist.

Assistant prosecutor Sheila Cummings was ready. She prepared her witnesses well— especially her star, Gordon Krone.
"Mr. Krone, you did a good job last time, so I am not criticizing;
however, this time we really have to bring it home to the jury

that you are absolutely positive the man you saw in the 7-Eleven is the defendant. There can be no doubt conveyed to the jury. Okay?" Sheila was going way over the ethics line again in the preparation of her witness.

"I understand, Ms. Cummings, and I thank you for the transcript of my previous testimony. It will prove helpful to me." Gordon was looking forward to testifying. *I'll show all these lawyers and everybody who reads the papers just what Gordon Krone is made of. Reject me for a law enforcement job, will ya? Serves you right!*

A jury was chosen in just two days. Sheila and Avery delivered their opening statements, neither having strayed much in nature from that of the first trial. Sheila decided to take Gordon Krone's testimony sooner than in the first trial. She planned to put Gordon on just after Gilhooley and Dr. Restin, and then follow up with the expert on blood analysis. Her reasoning was Gordon's testimony would have a better impact on the jury if heard early on. The witnesses who would testify about Callie's affair with Johnny Campbell and Boyd's with Alice Moore would be called a little later. In that way, motive would be the last the jury would hear from her.

Avery tried to assure Boyd, "Mack and the guys did a great job, Boyd. Under normal circumstances, we would go to the prosecutor and work toward a criminal case against Krone. In this case, all we can prove right now is the insurance fraud, and that's not enough to help you. We need to blow the roof off the courthouse, in front of the press, and show this guy for what he is. Mack, Worten and Higgins are all hard at work trying to pull it together, and my hope is they will bring it in before Krone testifies."

There's nothing in the rules that either attorney has to advise the other of the order of witness testimony, so when Sheila called Gordon to the stand, it was a surprise to Avery. With Sheila guiding him, Gordon's testimony was even more demonstrative than in the first trial.

When it came time for cross-examination, Avery pushed hard on his time-based reasoning. "Mr. Krone, I still cannot grasp how anyone could have the recall you claim, given the admitted short time you were allegedly in the defendant's presence in the 7-Eleven and the admitted long time between that incident and when you saw him on television. Can you explain that to the jury?"

"Sure, I can." Gordon stole a fleeting glance at Ms. Cummings. "Whenever I run into a situation that calls for quick thinking, I rely on my law enforcement training and the experience I had as a corrections officer." He was confident. He turned to the jury. "Whenever I find myself in an awkward situation—like bumping into someone—my senses elevate. It's almost like turning on a camera in my mind. My recall is very precise. I am sure of what happened on that day in the 7-Eleven. I am also positive it was the defendant." With that last line, he pointed at Boyd Richards.

A stir in the back of the courtroom caused Avery to turn around. Prosecutor Lant had entered, as had Chief Worten, Mack and Higgins. While the others took seats, Mack walked up the center aisle and handed a note across the wooden balustrade separating the gallery from the front of the courtroom. Avery read the short note and rose. "Your Honor, could we have a short recess? I am not finished with this witness."

Judge Thomas replied, "You have fifteen minutes, Mr. Reddy. The witness will remain in the courtroom. The jury will retire until called upon."

Sheila gave a summoning heads-up to Gordon. He went over to her table, as the jury filed out. He asked, "What's that all about?"

"I don't know. Probably another theatric event by Mr. Reddy," she said dismissively, but the presence of Prosecutor Lant gave her pause.

"Are you sure? Absolutely sure?" asked Avery in the small conference room down the hall. He couldn't believe what lay before him wrapped neatly in evidence bags. "Let's go back in and fry this sonovabitch!"

"If you are ready to proceed, Mr. Avery, I will recall the jury." Judge Thomas nodded to the bailiff and settled into his leather chair. "Mr. Krone, please take the witness stand. You are still under oath. Mr. Reddy, you may continue."

"Thank you, Your Honor. Just a few new questions, Mr. Krone." He looked over at Sheila and repeated, "and I do mean *new* questions."

Avery fingered the cardboard box on the defense table given to him by Mack. He rose and approached Gordon. "Mr. Krone, do you know Harlan Getz?"

"No, I do not!" Gordon's shock was obvious. He looked over at Sheila wide-eyed. She frowned and rose.

"Objection, Your Honor. What does this have to do with cross-examination?"

"Mr. Avery?"

"Your Honor, I need a little latitude on this, but the court will see, not only where I am going, but the need for it. Please bear with me."

"Okay, but you'd better not be wasting the court's time. I may be new, but I will not hesitate to sanction an attorney fooling with my patience." The judge peered over his glasses for effect.

"Thank you, Your Honor. Mr. Krone, you don't know Harlan Getz? Okay, how about Bruce Harrington, Willis Hampton, John Cassidy, David Williams... shall I go on?"

"Objection. Your Honor, can we do away with the census inquiry?" Sheila's objection was a matter of form, but she was aghast when she looked over at Gordon. He was swaying from side to side, his glazed eyes staring at the ceiling.

"Just one more, Your Honor." Before the judge could respond, Avery reached into the box and held up a plastic bag containing a large hunting knife. "Recognize this, Mr. Krone, or whatever your name is today?"

It started as a communal gasp in the courtroom and became a loud buzz of voices questioning what had just occurred. Judge Thomas banged his gavel repeatedly to no avail. The bailiff tried to calm everyone, but no one paid him any mind, either.

Prosecutor Raymond Lant rose from the back of the court room and, in his long and lanky manner, walked down the center aisle. His deep voiced penetrating the din, he said, "Your Honor, may I approach as a 'Friend of the Court?'"

"You may, Mr. Lant, but first this jury will leave the room, and I mean pronto!"

The courtroom gradually regained its decorum, everyone hanging on each word the prosecutor spoke. "Your Honor, for some time members of my office and others have been investigating new leads in this case. Unfortunately, up until this morning nothing had materialized. New evidence produced by the defense team and presented to me, personally," he paused and glowered at Sheila Cummings, "caused me to request a search warrant for the residential trailer of Gordon Krone. We have found irrefutable evidence that Gordon Krone murdered an insurance claims person, Harlan Getz, which led to the murder of Callie Richards when she encountered him just after he killed Getz. Also, we can prove that Krone murdered one Johnny Campbell, believing him to be a threat. Mr. Reddy, please show Mr. Krone the rope segment we found in his trailer." In disgust, he added, "The rope, like the knife, is another sick trophy, no doubt."

At this point, Gordon Krone was in another zone. His hands were against the rail, and though still seated, he was mimicking pushups, his face contorted in a weird smile.

Chief Bill Worten walked over to Gordon with the bailiff. "Gordon Krone, you are under arrest for the murder of Callie Richards—for starters." He read Gordon his rights, but Gordon was on another wavelength.

Prosecutor Lant leaned over the prosecution table and whispered to the assistant prosecutor, "Sheila, you might want to give Congressman Barrett a call and see if he has any work for you. I surely don't!" Sheila's head was bowed.

Boyd Richards broke down, as Avery stood behind him gripping the sobbing man's shoulders. Mack, Higgins and Chief Worten exchanged happy victory faces. Higgins said, "It's really nice when something comes together, ain't it? Just like Yogi says, 'The game ain't over till it's over.'"

Her producer cued her. "This is Marsha Gruener reporting to you again on the Boyd Richards murder trial. I am standing outside Courtroom Number One on the second floor of the Union County Courthouse in Elizabeth, New Jersey. Well, Tom, a remarkable thing just happened behind those doors you see back there. Defense Counsel Avery Reddy was halfway through his cross-examination of one of the state's witnesses, Gordon Krone, when he exposed the *witness* as the alleged killer of Callie Richards. Not only that, the man was arrested on the spot, right in the courtroom. Following an explanation by Prosecutor Raymond Lant, Judge Thomas dismissed the murder complaint against Boyd Richards on the spot. Our viewers will recall that Boyd Richards was an unsuccessful candidate for New Jersey's Seventh Congressional District. Quite an exciting end to what was a sensational trial all along. This is Marsha Gruener for NBC News. Back to you in the studio, Tom."

EPILOGUE

*T*he **corrections officer was droning on** about regulations and in-house punishment, but all Krone could think about were his pushups. His biceps ached for lack of the usual punishment he inflicted on them. Finally, his inmate group arrived at the cell assignment desk. Actually, it was a window where the new inmate would step up and give his name and number, then be given a card with a cell number on it.

"Krone, Gordon, sir. Number 5164439," he informed the sergeant at the desk behind the glass.

The sergeant had hardly looked up during the past fifteen inmates he processed, but now he jerked to attention and gazed over the top of his reading glasses. "Can it really be you? Am I that lucky to get you on the flip side, Krone?"

"Yup, it's me sergeant. I wasn't sure you'd remember me." Krone's response was friendly and offered with a broad smile.

The sergeant's face reddened. He jumped to his feet behind the glass and hollered, "You piece of crap! You know better than to speak in the line." He drew closer to the window—his voice lowered, but anger far from diminished—and said, "Oh, I remember you...you, wuss!

Couldn't make it on the outside either, huh? Maybe your classmates here should know you used to be a C.O., huh?" He settled back and smiled wickedly. "Well, we're gonna take really good care of you in here." Shaking his head and still smiling, he waved Krone off. "Next?"

The young corrections officer took over and guided Krone to his cell. The cell door was ajar, and inside a small pale man with glasses looked up from his book and smiled. He rose and offered Krone his hand, saying, "My name is Bill Conklin, but they call me Chip. I'm in for insurance fraud, but I'll be out in a few months. Small beef, ya know? What did they hit you with?"

Krone sank onto the edge of the lower bunk, and with his head down, he grumbled, "I'm here for insurance fraud, too, but it got a little complicated."

"Please, everyone, may I have your attention." Boyd Richards was at the head of the table with his glass raised. "I want to propose a toast: First, to a lawyer's lawyer—no pun intended—Avery Reddy. You believed in me and kept me bolstered up when I needed it most. But, more, you knew when to change gears and go in an unorthodox direction. There are a lot of skilled lawyers out here, but not many who can put aside convention and think outside the box. Thank you, Avery!" Then Boyd added jokingly, "Even if you did have to be dragged kicking and screaming to the truth!" He said that with a deferential glance at Mack and Higgins.

The group of friends met in Michelino's Restaurant on Washington Avenue in Elizabeth. Along with Boyd Richards,Avery Reddy, Prosecutor Raymond Lant and his wife, Veronica; Chief Bill Worten; Mack and Penny; Bob and Brenda Higgins; and Nezzie sat around the table. They had just finished eating, and a round of after-dinner drinks was arriving.

Boyd Richards wasn't done. "I also want to toast my friend, Raymond Lant. You never stopped believing in me. Without a doubt, the unorthodox investigation team of Bill Worten, Mack Mackey, his secretary, Inez, and Bob Higgins saved me. You all worked your tails off to make today happen, and I am forever in your debt. I can only imagine what would have happened to me had you all not pulled together and, not only proved my innocence; but caught Callie's killer, as well. " He hesitated a moment, then with tears welling, he stated, "I know my Callie forgives me as I do her." His voice cracking, he finished. "I think I better sit down."

As always happens, multiple conversations broke out around the table. Mack asked the prosecutor, "What's goin' on with Krone? Has anyone gotten anything from him?"

Prosecutor Lant shook his head in disgust. "You won't believe this: I am told he is acting out an insanity defense, claiming he suffers from dissociative identity disorder or what we used to call multiple personality disorder. His attorney hired a psychiatrist who claims it was Krone's other identities that committed the crimes, and *he* is the victim. Something about being locked in a closet when he was a kid."

"Good luck with that one!" Bob Higgins offered. "He does the research, gets fake driver's licenses, addresses, bank accounts, and uses disguises to hide his real identity. Then he methodically kills three people to avoid detection. Sounds like premeditation to me, not the work of someone helplessly led by compulsion."

Mack stoically remarked, "It's too bad three innocent people had to die so this self-indulged misfit tries to avoid prosecution for insurance fraud. For what... a six-month prison tour, at most? All three victims were nothing more than loose ends. What a shame."

Two hours later and back in Mack's apartment, he and Penny were having a tickling good time. First, he—then she—had the upper hand, rolling around and giggling on the carpet. "Listen, Mack, you and I have our own 'loose end' to take care of, ya know?"

"Well, it's not loose anymore," he said, sheepishly.

She whispered in his ear, "I noticed."

END

"ACCIDENTAL P.I."

A memoir by David B. Watts

Have you ever wondered what it would be like to be a real-life private investigator watching the bad guys through binoculars during a surveillance or interviewing witnesses in a murder investigation? Or, how about seeing yourself testifying in a big federal court case? Maybe you could envision yourself conducting a corporate corruption investigation for some of the Fortune 500 companies. Your author, David B. Watts, has done all of those things and is pleased to share many of them with you in his first book, *Accidental P.I.*, also published by North Loop books.

As a real-life private investigator, David's life story treats you to these experiences and more. Unlike P.I. work as portrayed in the movies and on television, *Accidental P.I.* offers a peek behind-the-scenes showing how investigators really get the job done.

New York Times best-selling author, Randy Wayne White, says, "*I thoroughly enjoyed Accidental P.I. by David B. Watts. It is a series of tales that are all-the-more compelling because they are fact, not fiction, although Watts writes with the skill of a novelist.*"

Accidental P.I. is available at Barnes & Noble, Amazon.com, eBooks, and the author's website, www.accidentalpi.com.

ABOUT *the* AUTHOR

*D*avid B. Watts has been a licensed private investigator for the past four decades, specializing in fraud and business investigations. He and Linda, his wife of 55 years, worked for major law firms, insurance companies and the Fortune 500 in the busy New York to Philadelphia corridor on cases ranging from kickbacks to special security issues. David has also worked half-a-dozen murder cases and innumerable insurance fraud matters. Authenticity comes through in his writing after a lifetime of experience, and he shares that with his readers.

His investigation career began in his twenties as a Plainfield, New Jersey patrolman. He was promoted to detective, then joined the Union County Prosecutor's Office as a county investigator. These early experiences eventually launched him into a lifelong career in private sector investigation work. His pursuit of the facts brought him into state and federal courts as well as the board rooms of major corporations. He is respected among his peers and continues to take on special investigations, now in his seventies. David also offers power point presentations to civic groups, libraries and businesses on the enormously current topic of identity theft.

Sincerest Thanks

*A*gain, I thank my compassionate editor and bookstore owner, Susie Holly. She forgives me for over-using and abusing ellipses (...) and em dashes (—). It is apparent I lack "comma sense" when it comes to these neat means of expression in dialogue. Visit her great little book store, MacIntosh Books and Paper, should you find yourself on Sanibel Island, Florida.

For agreeing to be in the book as themselves, and for their years of friendship and business association, Bob & Brenda Higgins deserve more than a simple-thanks. B&B, as I call them, are the greatest!

Dr. P. Denis Kuehner, our family physician when in Florida, listened patiently to some of the medically related passages in the book and offered helpful suggestions. Thanks, "Doc."

For reading the final pre-production draft and giving her enthusiastic support for my project I thank Anne Marie Gibson of Califon, New Jersey.

Thanks to Ralph Steele, a retired instructor at Mountainside Correctional Institute, a prison facility in Annandale, New Jersey. Ralph checked me out regarding "life on the inside."

The Harper Book of Quotations cannot be overlooked, as well. You didn't think I knew all those cool quotations myself, did you?

Madeline O'Malley, a friend and former paralegal, added her insight as an avid reader of court room and criminal drama stories.

Carlos Perez—another friend on Sanibel Island. Florida—read the first rough draft and gave me a thumb's up in between customers at the Sunset Grill.

Brian Wurdemann, a friend and cheerleader for my writing efforts, has my heartfelt thanks. His ongoing encouragement means a lot, as does his support for my identity theft project.

The helpful people at Mill City Press have been wonderful throughout the design, development and marketing of both books and I look forward to working with them again in the future.

Linda R. Watts, my loving bride of fifty-five years and counting, is always at and on my side. Her love and patience is deeply appreciated—especially when I am drifting around in creative space looking for the right word or phrase or struggling with a resistive paragraph.

Finally, I thank you, dear reader, for taking a chance on a new author. I hope you enjoyed our sojourn into murder in the New Jersey suburbs…more to come!